THE ROBOT ROAD TO FARAWAY

His was a dream few spacemen ever saw come true. Alan Kemp was an obsessed man – driven by the realization of a dream into the black emptiness between the stars.

In a rebuilt, second-hand, obsolete ship, Kemp and his three comrades took off – determined to set up a shuttle between the planets at the Rim of the galaxy.

But trouble – in the form of two lost colonies, one inhabited by giant mechanical insects and the other ruled by the descendants of a murderous pirate – threatened. Kemp's crew began to wonder: just how much will a man sacrifice to realize a dream?

When The Dream Dies

A. BERTRAM CHANDLER

SPHERE BOOKS LIMITED
30-32 Gray's Inn Road, London WC1X 8JL

First published in Great Britain by Allison & Busby Ltd 1981
Published by Sphere Books Ltd 1981

Original publication as RENDEZVOUS ON A LOST WORLD

To Scott Meredith

TRADE
MARK

Printed and bound in Great Britain by
©ollins, Glasgow

Chapter One

When the dream dies, what of the dreamer?

Chapter Two

It was Kemp's dream, although we shared part of it. It was Kemp's dream, but Jim Larsen participated in it, and Dudley Hill, and myself. It was a dream that is not uncommon among spacemen, especially such spacemen as ply their trade out and away from the well-serviced shipping routes. It was a dream that some few spacemen have made come true.

Alan Kemp, when I first met him, was Chief Officer of the old *Rimhound*. He was a typical enough Rim Runners officer inasmuch as he, like most of us in such employment, had served in big ships before coming out to the Rim. He retained a dignity, almost a pomposity of bearing that didn't match either the shabbiness of his uniform or the decrepitude of his vessel. For the rest, he was a big man, tall, grey-haired, and with the bleak blue eyes that spacemen always seem to own in fiction but so seldom do in fact. But he was, once you got to know him, once you got past his reserve, a good shipmate and a good friend. Had he not been so the rest of us would never have accompanied him in his venture.

Old Jim Larsen was *Rimhound*'s Second Interstellar Drive Engineer. We all called him 'Old Jim'. On meeting him for the first time, the impression of extreme age was the one that presented itself. But then you became aware of alertness, aliveness, of the somehow indestructible youth that looked out from behind his grey eyes. And this made nonsense of his bald head, withered frame and wrinkled face.

Nobody knew just how old he was. His Chief Interstellar Engineer Certificate had been folded and refolded so many times that the date of birth recorded on the piece of parchment was illegible. It was strongly suspected that this date was nothing like the one that he used when signing ship's Articles. Also, his Certificate carried an Ehrenhaft Drive endorsement, and the last of the Ehrenhaft Drive ships, the gaussjammers, was broken up before I was born.

Dudley Hill was Third Mate. Like Kemp, he had served in the big ships of the Interstellar Transport Commission. Unlike Kemp, he had not waited until he was a senior officer before he had resigned from the Commission's service. Rumour had it that he had been asked to resign, that he had been implicated in the collision of *Beta Scorpii* with an asteroid in the Rigellian planetary system.

Rumour had it, too, that he had been made the scapegoat and that *Beta Scorpii*'s Master, who possessed powerful friends in the Commission's upper hierarchy, was responsible for the error of judgement that resulted in the near-wreck. However, Rim Runners, chronically short of officers, asks no questions, and Dudley was as sober and reliable a spaceman as any on the Rim, and more so than most.

And myself? I was *Rimhound*'s Purser, the spacefaring office boy, as I was sometimes called. Like the others, I'd drifted out to the Rim. I was, rather more years ago than I care to remember, once in the Waverly Royal Mail. The

Waverly Royal Mail has rather old-fashioned ideas as to what constitutes gentlemanly conduct on the part of its officers. (The Kingdom of Waverly, of course, is the last stronghold of old-fashioned ideas.) The Waverly Royal Mail doesn't like divorce cases in which the evidence has been collected aboard one of its ships. The Waverly Royal Mail especially does not like Pursers who have been named as correspondents.

So . . .

Anyhow, we'd served together aboard *Rimhound* for some months. We'd got to know each other, had learned a great deal about each other's backgrounds. I'd met Alan's wife – he was the only one of the four of us who was married – quite a few times when the ship was in at Port Farewell, on Faraway, and each time I had envied Alan.

Veronica doesn't come into the story as a person, as a matter of fact, although her influence played a great part. Veronica was lovely. She was Carinthian, and if you've ever met a typical woman from that planet you'll be able to guess what she was like. I don't know why or how it is, but human stock on Carinthia seems to have mutated slightly, to have developed along the lines of the Siamese cat. That, I know, is biological nonsense, but it's the best way of giving an impression of the colouring of Carinthian women, the sleekness, the grace. If you like Siamese cats – and I do, and Alan did – you'll like the women of Carinthia.

Alan had met Veronica when she was travelling out to the Rim in the old *Delta Sextans*, of which vessel he was Chief Officer. He'd fallen for her, hard. He'd have been willing to have made his home on any planet of the galaxy as long as she was there, but I'm inclined to think that he was rather shaken when she announced her firm intention of living on Faraway. The Interstellar Commission doesn't maintain anything like a regular service to the

Rim and so, throwing away his years of seniority, Alan left them and joined Rim Runners.

So there we were, the four of us, in *Rimhound* when she was switched off the usual tramlines – the Lorn, Faraway, Ultimo, Thule and Eastern Circuit run – and chartered to the Shakespearian Line. It made a change. It was a plunge in towards the Centre, although not a very deep one. The Shakespearian Sector may not be officially regarded as part of the Rim, but it's so far out that the night skies of its worlds display only a sparse sprinkling of stars.

We carried a full cargo of agricultural machinery from Port Farewell, on Faraway, to Port Fortinbras, on Elsinore. It was our luck – bad luck, we thought at first – to arrive there in time for the beginning of the Cargo Handlers' strike, an industrial dispute that dragged on and on.

As a result of this long period of enforced idleness there was ample planet leave. And there was, too, ample time for those of us with wives and families to become more than usually browned-off with a means of livelihood that made long periods of separation inevitable, that entailed the occasional lengthening of such periods by the stubbornness of trade union leaders and employers of labour on distant worlds.

Of the four of us, Alan Kemp was the most browned-off. We were not surprised. We knew him well by this time, knew his moods, knew that even a month away from Veronica was, for him, little short of eternity. I know this much, too. If I'd been married to her my spacefaring days would have been over, even if the only shore employment offering had been shovelling sludge in the sewage conversion plant. But Alan was different.

Even so, there could have been far worse worlds for a holdup than Elsinore. It's a pleasant enough hunk of dirt. The land is mainly flat, and fertile and well wooded.

There are no extremes of temperature except at the Poles and at the Equator. There are almost no heavy industries. The people are an outwardly stolid breed, running to blondness and fatness, both men and women.

In spite of their stolidity, or because of it, they are inveterate gamblers. They gamble on the turn of a card, on the fall of a coin or the dice. They make wagers on horseraces, on dograces, on races between representatives of such of the indigenous fauna as are noted for fleetness of foot or wing. Every town, every village, even, boasts its casino. Then, to rake in such folding money as may still be floating around, there are private lotteries, and municipal lotteries, and state lotteries.

Oddly enough, none of us was a gambler. Come to that, we were rather deficient in all the vices – with the exception of old Jim Larsen – leading, by Rim Runners' standards, lives of quite exceptional virtue. But after a few weeks of Elsinore we began more and more to frequent the taverns in and around Fortinbras. Alan Kemp was not often one of the party. About once a week, however, he would declare that he had to get off the ship before he was driven even farther round the bend than he was already, and join us.

He was always rather a morbid drinker and liked to drink in morbid surroundings. When he was with us we invariably finished the evening at the Poor Yorick, an establishment justly famous for its funeral decor. We would sit around a coffin-shaped table drinking beer from mugs that were facsimiles of human skulls – they even had the horrid feel of old bone – listening to the fine selection of funeral marches that was the only music obtainable from the jukebox, the casing of which was the work of a monumental mason. The dim lighting was by flickering, smoking tallow candles. The floral decorations took the form of floral tributes.

The night that it all started, the night that the dream began to come true, Alan was in fine form. There had been a mail in that morning – the Commission's *Epsilon Crucis*, in-bound from the Rim – and there had been no letters for our Chief Officer. The inevitable result was that he was both sulking and worrying.

'Space,' he announced, for about the fifth time that evening, 'is no life for a civilised man.'

'You,' I told him, 'are not a civilised man. You know damn well that you could never settle down ashore. Ships are your life.'

'That might have been true,' he said, 'before I met Veronica. It's not true now.'

'Then why don't you just get the hell out of it?' asked Jim Larsen.

'Given a job that pays as well as this,' said Alan, 'I would.'

'You wouldn't,' I told him. 'You're too fond of being a big frog in a small puddle. You've been a senior officer too long, first in the Commission's ships, then with Rim Runners. And you think that you might as well stick it out and become Master now.'

'All right,' he said. 'Perhaps I do. But there's only one way to be really happy as Master, and that's to be an owner as well.' He sipped his beer thoughtfully. 'A little ship could be fitted in the Eastern Circuit without trampling on our revered employer's corns too heavily. A shuttle service, say, between Mellise and Grollor.'

'Even little ships cost big money,' pointed out Dudley Hill gloomily.

Old Jim laughed. 'This is the world to get it on. What about the lotteries? If you aren't in, you can't win.'

'The trouble is,' I told them, 'that money just can't be taken off Elsinore. Currency regulations and restrictions and all the rest of it.'

'Your point,' said Alan, 'is purely academic. Surely you know by this time that it is always somebody else who wins prizes in lotteries. I'll prove it.' He beckoned to the waiter, a cadaverous, black-clad individual. 'I suppose that you sell lottery tickets here?'

'Indeed, yes, sir. Tattersall's? Elsinore State? Fortinbras Municipal?'

'Which one is drawn the first?'

'Tattersall's, sir.'

'Then I'll have a ticket. A losing ticket.'

The man smiled. 'The *winning* ticket, sir.'

'Oh, no. If *I* hold it, it can't possibly win.'

'As you say, sir. That will be two dollars.'

'I'm prepared to pay to prove my point,' said Alan gloomily.

Two days later, he learned that he had won a hundred thousand Elsinore dollars.

Alan Kemp, like many others in like circumstances, had blandly assumed that all his worries would be over when he won the big prize. Like those others he soon discovered that his worries were just beginning.

'Until this moment,' he grumbled, 'I always thought that lack of money was my biggest trouble. Now I'm not so sure.'

'Come off it,' I told him. I looked at the solidograph of Veronica that stood on his desk, the figurine in the cube of clear plastic that seemed almost alive, that held all the grace and loveliness of her in miniature. 'Come off it, Alan. You've a beautiful wife and a not so small fortune. What the hell more do you want?'

'She,' he said patiently, 'is on Faraway. The fortune is here. On Elsinore.'

'There are such vehicles as passenger-carrying spaceships, you know. I can see no reason why the pair of you shouldn't settle on Elsinore. You could set yourselves up in some kind of business.'

'I've thought of that. But there's only one kind of business that we've ever dreamed of setting ourselves up in.'

'You mean what you were talking about the other night? Owner and Master?'

'Yes. As I was saying, a little ship with a minimal crew, paid on a share basis. Myself as Master and Veronica as Catering Officer – as you know, she's a first-class cook. Other people have made a go of it, on those lines. And now, when at last we have some capital to play with, there's no way of getting it off this blasted planet.' He splashed some more gin into our glasses. 'Are you sure there's no way, George?'

'Quite sure,' I said. 'I've spent all day exploring every avenue on your behalf, leaving no stone unturned. I started in Port Fortinbras. There's only one way for you to get the money off Elsinore, and that's to buy things for export to the Rim Worlds. And you haven't a hope in hell of doing that, not for a couple of years, at least. All available tonnage is booked up that far ahead.'

'There's always the odd *Epsilon*-class tramp drifting in,' he suggested, not very hopefully.

'And suppose one does? What chance do you stand against the local exporters, all clamouring for cargo space?'

'I could employ an Agent.'

'And he'd soon whittle your hundred thousand down to size. Seriously, Alan, why don't you and Veronica settle on Elsinore?'

He refilled our glasses, then filled and lit his foul pipe. He said, 'I've considered that. I'd be quite happy about it; as far as I'm concerned home is wherever Veronica is. But I'm pretty sure that she would never consent. You know, as well as I do, that there are two classes of people who come out to the Rim – although I suppose that most of us are sort of hybrids, belonging to both classes. There are those who come out to make a living, who think that there are better chances of advancement on the Rim Worlds than on the heavily populated planets of the Centre. Then there are those who come out for psychological reasons, who are running away from something, who are running away as far as they possibly can.'

'I never thought that Veronica came into that category.'

'She does. I met her, you know, when she was travelling out in the old *Delta Sextans* from Carinthia to Van Diemen's Planet. She had her passage booked right out to Faraway even then – Interstellar Transport Commission, Shakespearian Lines, Rim Runners, the usual. When we got to know each other she told me something of her life story, enough for me to be able to fill in details for myself.

'She and some man had contrived to make a stinking mess of each other's lives, so much so that she decided to make a clean break, to get out and clear, to get away as far as possible. I caught her on the rebound, I suppose. Or she caught me. And that's how and why I resigned from the Commission's service, to make a fresh start in these interstellar rust-buckets.'

'And she won't budge from the Rim?'

'No. Shortly after I first came out I was offered a command in the Shakespearian Line. I had to turn it down, even though I was only a bold Third Mate with Rim Runners at the time. To the Rim she's come, and on the Rim she'll stay. With me, or alone.'

'I had no idea,' I said, not entirely truthfully.

'When it comes to the inner workings, or the malfunctionings of a marriage,' he told me, 'outsiders rarely do.'

'I suppose not.'

'Some more gin?'

'No thanks. I'll be drinking you out of house and home.'

He grinned wryly. 'I can afford it.'

'All right then. But make it a small one.'

I saw him stiffen abruptly as he was pouring the drinks, his face suddenly alert. I wondered what was amiss and then heard, faintly, the wailing notes muffled by our hull insulation, the spaceport alarm siren.

Alan slammed down the bottle, jumped to his feet, ran out into the alleyway. I followed him, saw him clambering up the short ladder from the officers' flat to the control room. I called out, asking him what was wrong. He replied curtly that he didn't know. (He thought, as I did, he told me later, that there was some kind of civil commotion arising from the strike, that the spaceport was under attack by a mob.)

I was surprised and relieved to find, when I joined Alan at the big viewports, that all was apparently quiet, that the wide expanse of scarred concrete was deserted, that there was no unusual activity at or around the spaceport gates.

Chapter Three

The night was dark, clear overhead, but with a suggestion of mist at ground level. To the southward the lights of Fortinbras City were bright, casting their usual diffused glow into the sky but, as yet, the spaceport was almost without illumination. Atop the Control Tower the red light was flashing the warning signal that a ship was about to arrive or depart. But we were the only ship in port and our departure date was a matter for uninformed conjecture, and no other vessel was due for all of three weeks.

'I've been ringing the Port Captain,' Kemp told me, 'but every time that I've tried to get through the line's been engaged. Give it a go, will you? When you raise him, let me know.' He picked up a pair of powerful binoculars, stared through them up at the wide circle of night sky that was visible through the transparency at our stem.

I picked up the telephone – it was spaceport property and was connected by landline to the communications system of Elsinore – and punched the buttons for the Port Office number. After six fruitless attempts the screen lit up. From it glared the worried face of a man whom I recognised as one of the minor port officials. 'Yes?' he snapped. 'What do you want?'

'Officer in charge of *Rimhound*, here,' I told him, handing the instrument to Alan.

'What's all the flap about, Clancey?' Alan asked.

Faintly I heard the reply. 'Unidentified ship coming in. You'd better get that scow of yours off the field.'

'We can't. Main propellant pump's adrift for overhaul.'

'Then you'd better get all hands out of the ship and clear of the apron. The way the stranger's behaving, there's liable to be a mess when she hits.'

'Who is she?'

'Didn't you hear me say that she was unidentified? She's got no Deep Space radio; didn't send any signals until she was already within radar range. She's homing on our beacon, but she's coming in on an oblique trajectory, like an aircraft. That's all that I can tell you. Now get off the line.'

Alan looked at me, raised his eyebrows. 'Sound the general alarm, George,' he ordered. He put down the telephone, picked up the public address system microphone. He waited until I had released my pressure on the alarm button, until the bells had ceased, then said quietly,

'Your attention, please. This is the Chief Officer speaking. All hands are to evacuate ship immediately. All hands to evacuate ship. That is all.' He turned to me, said, 'That means us as well, George.'

'What do you think it is, Alan?'

'Probably purple pirates from the next galaxy but three. They'll be after my hundred grand. I told you that I just can't win.'

We scrambled down the short ladder from Control to the officers' flat, waited a few seconds for the cage of the little elevator to climb to us up the axial shaft, then dropped swiftly down to the after airlock, joining those few of our shipmates who, spending a quiet evening aboard, had been aroused by the alarm and by Alan's order to get out of the ship.

One of them, old Jim Larsen, asked, 'What is it, Alan?'

'I wish I knew,' Kemp told him. 'There seems to be some kind of unidentified spacecraft coming in like a bat out of hell, and the Port Captain's scared that she'll come a right royal gutser, so he wants us out of the ship and well clear of the apron when she hits.'

'Talking of bats out of hell,' remarked old Jim quietly.

The ground car that had roared through the spaceport gates braked to a skidding halt. The Old Man jumped out of the vehicle, that he had been driving himself, walked quickly to where we were standing.

'Mr Kemp! What's going on here?'

'Unidentified, unscheduled ship coming in for a landing. Orders from the Port Captain to get all hands away from the apron in case of a crash.'

'Then what are you still hanging around here for?'

'We owe a certain responsibility to *Rimhound*, sir.'

The Old Man smiled briefly. 'So we do, Mr Kemp. I feel that we should not stray too far from the ship until we know just what is happening.'

'We should have seen and heard rocket drive by now,' said somebody.

We heard the noise then, a low humming, a vibration rather than a sound, that seemed to be coming from above and from the north. We stared in that direction and saw, just before the field floodlights came on and dazzled us, something that was bathed in an eerie blue glow, something that expanded rapidly, with every passing second.

'Aliens?' whispered the Captain.

'No.' Old Jim's voice held assurance. 'No, Captain, but that's a sight that I thought I'd never see again in my lifetime, a sound that I thought I'd never hear again.'

'But what is it, man?'

'A gaussjammer. The last of the gaussjammers, it must be. A starship with the Ehrenhaft Drive.'

She came in fast, almost out of control, in what was, in effect, a shallow dive. She barely cleared the upthrusting spire that was *Rimhound*'s prow. The wind of her passage set the old ship rocking on her vanes and almost swept us off our feet. She struck the concrete midfield, the shape of her obscured by a fountain of ruddy sparks. To the shrieking of tortured metal she rushed on, until it seemed that she must crash into and wreck the Control Tower. Miraculously she slowed and stopped but not before she had ploughed up the ornamental lawn and shrubbery at the base of the administration buildings.

The arrival of the scurrying crashwagons, with their flashing red lights and wailing sirens, was something of an anti-climax.

We walked slowly towards the near-wreck, looking curiously at the deep, ragged furrow gouged out of the concrete. For some obscure reason I, at least, was more interested in the damage than in the machine that had caused it. I didn't look at the strange ship until we were almost up to her.

She was an odd-looking brute, her hull form conical, with the twisted remains of tripod landing gear around the sharp end of the cone. The other end, the base, although, obviously, it was the stem of the ship, was a shallow dome rather than a flat surface and was broken by large, circular observation ports. There was dim lighting inside the control room and we could see movement. And then, briefly, there was a pale face pressed against the transparency from within.

So the strangers were human.

'Keep back!' somebody was saying in an authoritative voice. I saw that it was Baines, the Port Captain. 'Keep back, you people. My rescue squad will be able to handle this.'

'Perhaps I can help,' suggested Jim Larsen.

'If I require any assistance I'll let you know,' snapped Baines.

'Do you know what sort of ship this is?' persisted old Jim.

'Obviously something new and experimental,' said Baines impatiently. 'Please don't waste any more of my time.'

'She's not new, Captain Baines. She's old. She's a gaussjammer, and I've served in the things. She's on her side now, and the airlock door is jammed. You'll have to roll her to get it clear.'

'Are you sure?' demanded Baines.

'I'm sure.'

In spite of his impatience Baines was willing to listen to reason, ready to make fresh decisions. It was for only a second or so that he stared at old Jim, then he called the chief of the rescue squad to his side. 'Mr Larsen knows this class of ship. Take orders from him, Harris.'

Harris did, setting up jacks and then, after they had done their work, parbuckling gear to Jim's instructions. Although the ship was small, little more than a yacht, she was amazingly heavy. Robust she must have been, we knew, to have survived her rough landing in such apparently good shape.

I remarked upon the excessive weight of her to Jim as the creaking tackles of the parbuckle were slowly turning her about her longitudinal axis.

'It's the soft iron,' he told me. 'Those ships used soft iron for almost everything. They had to.' He broke off to shout instructions to the winch drivers. 'Easy, there! Easy! There are people inside this thing, and some of them may be injured!'

Gradually the hair-thin circle of the airlock came into view, lifting clear of the heaped earth of the ruined garden. Larsen stepped forward, rapped smartly on the hull with a spanner. Answering raps sounded from inside.

Slowly, on creaking hinges, the door opened.

The man who emerged from the airlock was bleeding from a gash on his pale forehead, but, otherwise, seemed uninjured. He was in uniform, an elaborate rig of blue and gold with wide bands of gleaming braid on the sleeves, with massive, ornate epaulettes. He looked at us as curiously as we were looking at him, seemed to find our simple shorts and shirts lacking in dignity. His attention wavered between our Old Man, Captain Williams, and Captain Baines, each of whom wore on his shoulder boards the four gold bars of astronautical authority. He asked at last, with an unidentifiable accent, 'Who is in charge here?'

'I am the Port Captain,' said Baines.

'I, sir, am Admiral O'Hara of the Space Navy of

Londonderry. Some of my people were injured in the landing. I request that you afford medical and hospital facilities.'

'My rescue squad and ambulance men are standing by, Admiral. May they enter your ship?'

'They may.' O'Hara turned to a less elaborately uniformed officer standing inside the airlock. 'Commander Moore, will you see to the casualties? These men wish to bring their stretcher parties into the vessel.' He pivoted to face Baines again, a petulant frown on his heavy face. 'Port Captain, I wish to make a serious complaint.'

'Yes, Admiral?'

'I homed on your beacon, sir, only to find that your spaceport is situated nearer to your magnetic equator than to your magnetic pole. Surely, sir, it is obvious that any vessel obliged to make a landing in a locality where horizontal force is well in excess of vertical force will be, at least, seriously discommoded.'

'Too right,' agreed Larsen.

The admiral and the two captains glared at him, then Baines, breaking the short silence, addressed O'Hara. 'Are all your ships like this one, Admiral?'

'Of course, Port Captain. How else would one design and build an interstellar ship?'

'I am told,' Baines continued cautiously, 'that this vessel of yours is a gaussjammer.'

'That is, I believe, the slang name for starships.'

'Furthermore, this is the first gaussjammer that I have seen, although I have read about them in astronautical histories.' He was warming up now. 'Furthermore, I have never heard of, until this moment, the Republic or Kingdom or whatever it is of Londonderry, although I hope, most sincerely, that it will be able to foot the bill for the damage to my spaceport. Furthermore – '

He was interrupted by O'Hara's officer who, approaching the admiral, saluted smartly and reported, 'All casualties out of the ship, sir.'

'Thank you, Commander.' O'Hara, turning again to Baines, seemed to have lost a little of his aggressiveness. 'You were saying, Port Captain?'

'I suggest, sir,' said Baines coldly, 'that any further discussions take place in private. Will you accompany me to my office? And you, Captain Williams, if you will be so good. And your Chief Officer.' He paused. 'Yes, and Mr Larsen. It will be as well to have somebody who knows something about this Ehrenhaft Drive along.'

It was late when the Old Man, Kemp and Larsen returned to the *Rimhound*.

Captain Williams went straight to his quarters, Kemp and Larsen found me in my cabin where, with Dudley Hill, I was discussing the night's events.

'I'd like to be able to have a look round that thing,' Dudley was saying. 'It's bloody absurd the way that they're keeping an armed guard posted at the airlock.'

'The bold Third Mate might get his wish yet,' said Alan.

We looked up, saw the two of them standing in the doorway.

'You're back,' I said, not very brightly.

'A blinding glimpse of the obvious, George. If you ask us and pour us a drink – I didn't go much on the Port Captain's whisky – we'll tell you all about it.'

'All right. Come in. Sit down. Here's the bottle. Here are glasses. Now talk.'

Kemp relaxed as far as relaxation was possible in the inadequate folding chair, but I could see that under his assumed ease of manner he was tense, excited.

He said, 'It was quite a session in Baines' office. Once

we got that so-called Admiral primed on rotgut all we had to do was sit back and listen. Fascinating it was. Straight from the pages of a historical novel.

'As you must already have guessed, this Londonderry of his is one of the Lost Colonies. You know the story of them, of course. Way back in the good old days of the First Expansion a gaussjammer runs into a magnetic storm and is flung away to hell and gone off trajectory with, as like as not, a dead pile and no power for the flywheel and the Ehrenhaft jennies. Nobody has a clue as to where she is, but they start up the emergency diesels, get the Ehrenhaft Drive working after a fashion and carry on until they stumble upon a habitable planet, if they're lucky. If they aren't . . .'

'I wish,' I said, 'that I had a dollar for every Lost Colony novel I've read, for every Lost Colony movie I've seen.'

Alan glared at me and growled, 'Oh, all right. Anyhow, there was this *Lode Derry*, a big migrant ship, commanded by one Captain O'Hara. She was bound from Earth to Atlantia, and the magnetic storm threw her off the tramlines when she was in the vicinity of Procyon. When her crew got things more or less under control again she was hopelessly lost.

'So they started up their diesels, hoped that supplies would hold out (the internal combustion engines, of course, burn hydrocarbons that, otherwise, would be used for food) and went planet hunting. You know that sector between Bellamy's Cluster and the Empire of Weaverley that's supposed to be anti-matter? Well, it's not, not all of it. *Lode Derry*'s people were lucky enough to find a small family of half a dozen suns, each with attendant planets, of normal matter.

'They made a landing on one of the planets. They sweated and slaved, and bred enthusiastically, and in only a couple or three generations had achieved quite a fair technological civilisation. There was a bit of luck about it; apart from anything else, the ship carried as part of her cargo, a Thorwaldsen Incubator complete, so it was possible easily to build up population to the minimal figure, and beyond. Too, as a migrant ship she had carried a large number of skilled craftsmen and technicians.

'They worked hard, and they multiplied, and they expanded. They built ships – and the Ehrenhaft Drive, of course, was the only interstellar drive of which they knew – ships that were modelled upon, although they were much smaller, *Lode Derry*. (They don't seem to have been very inventive people.) They colonised the other planets, the worlds revolving around the other suns of their tiny cluster.

'They learned by bitter and expensive experience, that they were marooned on a little island in the middle of a vast sea of anti-matter. How far this sea extended they did not know. They might even, they thought, have been flung clear out of this galaxy into another one. So they settled down, made the best of things. And then a magnetic storm threw O'Hara and his *Lode Derry* out and clear.'

'This Admiral business . . .' the Third Mate started to say.

'Oh, *that*. It's a hereditary rank, apparently. The first O'Hara – Captain O'Hara – sort of promoted himself when he became boss cocky of the colony. His descendants hold the title, and the honour and glory, without much power to go with it. The general idea is to give them a little ship and to let them play happily by themselves in some quiet corner. O'Hara isn't much of a spaceman and his crew are playboys like himself. O'Hara doesn't mind if he never sees Londonderry again and has already appointed himself Ambassador at Large to the rest of the galaxy. O'Hara will be happy to do any further space travelling as a passenger.'

'Where will he get the money to pay his fares?' I asked, the Purser in me coming to the surface.

'Once he gets to the Centre,' said Alan, 'he'll be sitting pretty. It's a long time since a Lost Colony was found, so he'll get the full prodigal son treatment.'

'He has to get to the Centre first,' I said. 'And it's an expensive business. And he has to live while he's on Elsinore. And the Elsinorians aren't notorious for either hospitality or generosity.'

'He can sell his ship,' said Alan.

'To whom? She might be of some value as a museum piece, but Elsinore doesn't run to an astronautical museum.'

'To me,' said Alan quietly.

'To you? But you don't know the first thing about her.'

'I'll remind you that I hold a Master Astronaut Certificate.'

'But that covers Mannschenn Drive and rockets, not some crazy, obsolete system of induced magnetism and flywheels.'

'I already have a Chief Engineer to handle that side of it,' he stated, nodding towards old Jim, who grinned in acknowledgement. 'As for the navigation, if an un-spaceman-like clod like O'Hara can cope, I can.'

'But O'Hara didn't cope. That's how he finished up here.'

'Magnetic storms are almost unknown on the Rim.'

'Almost. And, in any case, the Old Man will never release you.'

'He will, George, as long as I can supply substitutes. That shouldn't be hard. On every planet there are ex-spacemen who're crazy enough to feel the urge to make just one more trip.'

‘Substitutes? With an *s*? Plural?’

‘You heard me. There’ll be an engineer to replace old Jim, of course, and a new Second Mate – Petersen will be moving up one to take my place. And a new Third Mate.’

‘But I shall be the new Second Mate,’ Dudley pointed out in a pained voice. ‘There’ll be a row if I’m not.’

‘I was hoping,’ Alan told him, ‘that you’d be coming with me as Mate. No salary, of course, but shares . . .’

‘I rather think,’ said the Third, a slow smile spreading over his boyish features, ‘that you’ve talked me into it. You know, I was getting just a little bored with Rim Runners.’

‘And I’d rather like a Purser,’ Alan went on. ‘Preferably one who knows all the Agents and shippers along the Rim and the Eastern Circuit.’

‘All right,’ I said resignedly. ‘One of the clerks in the Agent’s office here wants to ship out as Purser. But, before we burn too many boats and count too many chickens before they’re hatched – will O’Hara sell?’

‘He’ll sell all right. The only thing that worries me is that he wants too damn much for that antique of his. There’ll have to be something left over for repairs and modifications.’

‘And,’ I added, ‘palm greasing.’

Chapter Four

Palm greasing there was.

As a Purser of long standing I thought that I knew all that there was to be known about that ancient and not-so-honourable art. As a shipowner – like the others, I was being paid in shares of the enterprise – I soon discovered that I didn't know the half of it. It was the certificates of clearance and spaceworthiness that were the most expensive, especially since, insofar as the astronautical regulations of Elsinore were concerned, there was no legal recognition of the Ehrenhaft Drive.

Lloyd's, by the way, never did get around to affording us coverage. *They* knew all about the Ehrenhaft Drive, it having been high on their black list for years. Furthermore, only starships with Mannschenn Drive can be fitted with the Carlotti communication and position-finding equipment; time-twisting radio devices are useless unless the vessel carrying them can be maintained in phase. So, not unreasonably, the underwriters considered that we, out of touch with the galaxy whilst *en route* and unable to avail ourselves of the latest navigational aids, would be altogether too heavy a risk.

But before there were all these troublesome details to worry us there were the formalities of the sale to conclude. We had cause to bless the currency regulations of Elsinore; had O'Hara been able to take his money with him when he left the planet he would, it is certain, have stuck out for a far higher price. As it was, he was able to buy a small hotel on the outskirts of Port Fortinbras with what was left over after the passages of himself and his entourage to Earth had been booked.

His aide, Commander Moore, who had had Space in a big way, even as a passenger, was installed there as manager, the idea being that the place would be a home for the so-called Admiral in the unlikely event of his returning to this sector of the galaxy.

Frankly, I rather envied the Commander and told Alan that if he had any sense at all he would have done the same, bringing Veronica to Elsinore to help him run the establishment. I told him I would willingly have served as barman. But he refused to listen to reason. His dream was coming true, and his dream belonged to the black emptiness between the stars, not to the warmth and light and comfort of any planetary surface.

Meanwhile, Alan and old Jim Larsen had their share of technical worries. To begin with, it was practically impossible for a ship fitted with Ehrenhaft Drive to lift from Port Fortinbras. I never really understood the whys and wherefores of it, but this was the way in which they explained it to me:

The Ehrenhaft Generators do not generate electricity; they generate a magnetic current, a flow of free magnetic particles. The ship becomes, in effect, herself a huge magnetic particle, strength and polarity of field as determined by her Captain. Like poles mutually repel – and so she lifts along the lines of magnetic force, repulsion and attraction being maintained in nice adjustment so as to avoid too fast an ascent with consequent overheating of the hull by atmospheric friction.

Once she is clear of the atmosphere, once she is on the right tramlines for her destination, her actual speed is utterly fantastic. Over relatively short distances, as within a planetary system, there is almost no time lag. But a Mannschenn Drive ship is controllable throughout her voyage; an Ehrenhaft Drive ship is not. It was this lack of control that made the gaussjammers so expensive, both in lives and material.

But I'm drifting away from the point, which is this: Port Fortinbras is situated far closer to the Magnetic Equator than to either of the Poles. The lines of force, therefore, are more nearly horizontal than vertical. A take-off, using the Ehrenhaft Drive, would have damaged the ship just as badly as did her landing.

The first plan, briefly considered, was to dissemble the vessel and to remove her, piece by piece, to a site not far from one of the magnetic poles, then and there to rebuild her. There were two drawbacks to this scheme. First there was the expense and second, all the Rim World spaceports are as unsuitable to a gaussjammer's requirements as is Port Fortinbras. And, for the ship to make any show at all of paying for herself, she had to be able to make use of existing port facilities.

The second plan was also expensive, but it was practicable. It entailed the conversion of *Lucky Lady* to an odd sort of hybrid rig. She remained, insofar as interstellar drive was concerned, a gaussjammer, but she was fitted with auxiliary rocket drive, her pile being modified so as to be able to flash-heat fluid propellant into incandescent gas. The theory of it was that she would lift on reaction drive and, at the same time, drift north or south to regions of more favourable magnetic declination. Once these had been reached she would switch over to Ehrenhaft Drive. The same procedure, but in reverse, would be used during landing operations.

To me it sounded very complicated. Kemp, Larsen and Hill all assured me that it wasn't. To me it all sounded very expensive, and nobody was prepared to argue with me about that. By the time that *Lucky Lady* was ready for Space she had eaten up all of Alan's hundred thousand dollars, together with the balance of wages with which the four of us had paid off from *Rimhound*.

Dreams are cheap enough. It's when you try to convert them into reality that they come dear.

The strike finished at last, as strikes do, and *Rimhound* completed discharge, commenced and completed loading, blasted off for the Rim Worlds, taking with her our old shipmates and the substitutes who had been engaged to fill the vacancies. O'Hara and his men shipped out in *Waltzing Matilda*, one of the tramps owned and operated by the Sundowner Line, for Zealandia, on the first leg of their long voyage towards the Centre. We weren't at all sorry when they left. *Rimhound*'s people had been very helpful to us, working with us on the conversion job, whereas O'Hara had just hung around like a bad smell, deploring all the horrid things that we were doing to his beautiful ship.

And then, not long after *Rimhound*'s departure, we were ready.

Lucky Lady was fuelled and stored and as spaceworthy as she ever would be. We had certificates, issued by all the competent authorities, excepting Lloyd's, to prove it. The newly installed rocket motors – but neither the motors nor the propellant pumps were new – had passed the static tests, had lifted the ship the regulation two hundred miles clear of the surface and then had lowered her gently to her berth. (One very large item of expense was the construction of a temporary blast wall to protect the administration buildings from our exhaust when we lifted from the berth that the ship had dug for herself during her uncontrolled, uncontrollable landing.)

Algae tanks and tissue culture vats, thanks to the generosity of *Rimhound*'s Catering Officer, were coming along nicely. The Ehrenhaft Generators, so we were assured by old Jim Larsen, were running sweetly. The two navigators, after a stint of really high-pressure study, reckoned that they were well able to cope with their art as practised in gaussjammers.

All bills were paid. All papers were in order. Contact had already been made with commercial interests on the worlds of the Eastern Circuit. And, better still, we had been able to pick up cargo – only a handful, but enough so that the voyage would show a tiny profit – from Elsinore to Faraway.

This suited all of us, and suited Alan Kemp most of all. Already he had been far too long away from Veronica, a period of separation made more irksome by the fact that she did not seem to be in a communicative mood, his frequent spacegrams being either unanswered or accorded only curt acknowledgement. But now, the Ehrenhaft Drive being what it was, there was quite a fair chance that he would be home some days before *Rimhound*. Furthermore, he would be returning as Master and owner, would be able to bring her on board and install her in the quite luxurious owner's suite, in comfort that it would be hard to buy ashore.

We had a little party in that same suite before blasting off. It wasn't a real party since there were only the four of us – or five, if you count the almost alive solidograph of Veronica that was standing on one of the tables – and we had only one glass of wine each.

'To the *Lucky Lady*,' said Alan, raising his glass.

'To *your* lucky lady,' I said, bowing to the little figurine in its cube of clear plastic.

'And now,' remarked Alan conversationally, 'it's high time that I was getting back to her.'

I was allowed to ride in the control room when we lifted from the surface of Elsinore. The ship, overmanned as she had been before the change of ownership, suffered from no shortage of acceleration chairs in that compartment. Alan, of course, was pilot. Dudley was co-pilot. I was in charge of communications.

'*Lucky Lady* to Spaceport Control,' I said, trying to make my voice calm and matter-of-fact. '*Lucky Lady* to Spaceport Control. Request permission to proceed. Over.'

'Spaceport Control to *Lucky Lady*. Proceed at will. Good luck to you. Over.'

I looked at Alan. He nodded. 'Thank you, Spaceport Control,' I said. 'Proceeding. Over.'

We proceeded.

We climbed upstairs like a homing drunk dreading his wife's reception of him. I tried to cheer myself up by remembering that the ship had passed all spaceworthiness tests, then remembered what one of the more notorious pessimists at Rim Runners had once told me: 'A test of any kind of gear proves only that the gear is working at the time of the test. Furthermore, such a test may well be the penultimate straw, the straw just before the last one that breaks the camel's back.'

I looked at Alan and Dudley again, looked at the instrument panel before them. Neither of them seemed unduly worried. There were white lights and green lights and amber lights on the panel, but no red ones. I looked away from them, out of the wide viewport. I was amazed to find that Elsinore was already hidden from view, that we had pierced the layer of cirro-stratus that had covered the sky that morning, were already well above a seemingly solid, desolate snowscape.

The ship was labouring less heavily. After all, I thought, she was not built, as were the ships to which we were accustomed, for handling under rocket power in a planetary atmosphere; there had been no need to design her hull form in accordance with the principles of aerodynamics. Now that she was almost clear of the gaseous envelope she would handle better, but once she was clear there would be no further need of the reaction drive.

Dudley Hill had swivelled in his seat so that he was facing a huge, transparent globe; a globe in which, at the touch of a button, there was blackness and the tiny specks of light that were stars. He touched another button, and curving filaments of luminosity sprang into being between the sparkling points.

'Captain,' he said, 'we've struck it lucky. We've hit the

tramlines for the Faraway Sun without any need for shunting.'

'Are you sure, Dudley?'

'See for yourself.'

The muffled thunder of the rockets died. I heard a jangling bell, saw that Larsen, from his engineroom, had replied on the telegraph to Kemp's order: *Stand By Ehrenhaft Drive*. The little model of the ship on the control panel suddenly glowed with violet light. I heard the whine and felt the vibration of the big flywheel starting up, the low humming of the Ehrenhaft Generators.

Alan was manipulating the vernier controls on the board before him. The violet light suffusing the translucent model changed suddenly to red. There was no shock, no sensation of dimensional distortion. But when I looked again through the viewport Elsinore and the Hamlet Sun had vanished; astern there was utter darkness and ahead the sky was a blaze of light. It was as though we were heading for the heart of some impossibly dense cluster instead of out towards the lonely Rim.

Alan relaxed in his chair, produced and filled and lit his pipe.

'So far, so good,' he said.

Dudley Hill did not relax. 'Did you say that magnetic storms were of rare occurrence out here?' he asked.

We looked into the transparent sphere, saw with horror that the once orderly lines of force were now a tangle of luminous spaghetti. It was then that the alarm bells started to ring, their urgent clangour drowning the dying whine of generators and gyroscope.

Lucky it was for us that Larsen had Ehrenhaft Drive experience, and luckier still that he had served in one of the few gaussjammers to have been thrown off course by a magnetic storm whilst still making a safe return to port. He knew the drill that had been worked out in theory and, better still, had seen the same drill put into practice.

He came up to the control room – dark save for the dimming emergency lights and the faint radiance of the sparse scattering of stars outside – and said, without preamble, 'I want to help.'

'Don't we all?' asked Dudley Hill.

Jim ignored him, saying to Alan, 'We have to start the emergency generators, the diesels. There's not enough juice left in the batteries to kick them over. It will have to be done manually.'

'There's no mad rush, I take it?' inquired Alan. 'What about your report first?'

'All right, Alan. Here's your report. Chief Engineer to Master . . .' He paused. 'Of course, if you don't mind waiting, I'll give it to you in writing. In quintuplicate.'

'No need to be funny, Jim.'

'No? Anyhow, who started it?' demanded the engineer, glaring at Dudley.

'Let's have the bloody report!' roared Alan.

'All right. The Pile's a lump of useless lead. The emergency batteries are damn near drained. Your ship is little more than a derelict. However . . .'

'Go on.'

'All we can do is start the diesels. They'll drive the emergency jenny. That'll drive one of the Ehrenhaft jennies, with a few loose electrons left over for heat and lighting.'

'And navigational equipment?'

'Yes, if you cut down on luxuries.'

'Then where do we go from here?'

'That's up to you, Alan. You're the navigator. As soon as the power comes back on your pretty chart, just pick a set of tramlines you fancy and proceed along it.'

'But where to?'

'That's up to you, Alan. Now, these diesels – who's going to give me a hand?'

'I'll come,' I said.

It was obvious that I was quite useless in the control room.

I followed Larsen along the spiral ramp to the engineroom – gaussjammers, of course, have no axial shaft. I looked dubiously at the sinister, dull-gleaming shape of the big generator that seemed to stir and shift ominously in the flickering light of the oil lamp. Following Larsen's instructions, I took the starting handle in both hands, tried to swing it. But starting a reluctant internal combustion engine, manually, in Free Fall conditions, is far from easy. At last I managed to twine both legs around a stanchion so that I had some purchase. The engine wheezed and coughed without enthusiasm, coughed again as though it almost meant it, and then, with startling suddenness, thudded into throbbing life.

Lights came on. Larsen went to the main switchboard, knocking up switches. 'Can't afford luxuries,' he grumbled. Then, on the other side of the engineroom, one of the spidery, flimsy-seeming Ehrenhaft Generators began to whisper to itself, its complexity of glittering parts stirring into motion. The whisper deepened to a drone, then shrilled to a high-pitched whine.

'That's that,' Jim muttered. 'Fuel enough for a few hours, but somebody had better get busy converting surplus hydrocarbons into more fuel. Anyhow, let's get back to Control and see how they're making out.'

We got back to Control.

We found that the navigational equipment was working again, that the big sphere that was the chart was once again a pretty picture of coloured sparks of light linked by glowing filaments.

It was a pretty picture, but, as was the picture that we could see from the viewports, a meaningless one.

We pushed on towards the nearer of the stars glowing in our chart tank. We sped along the tracks that led not from A to B, but from X to Y. And the star, a white dwarf, possessed no family of planets. Neither did the next star, nor the next, and the fourth one was circled only by a dark companion that must itself have been a dead star.

We pushed on, while rations became shorter and the ship's atmosphere more foul, both hydrocarbons and oxygen being gulped by the ravenous diesels. We pushed on, barely conscious at the finish, kept from slipping into a deep, permanent sleep only by the blinding headaches that afflicted us.

We pushed on, at last awakening from our daze to stare through the big telescope at the planet that swam in the blackness ahead of us. It was a fair world. Too fair, we feared, to be true. It was a world with a cloudy atmosphere, with breaks in the clouds through which we could make out sea and continent, mountain and prairie, blue water and green forest. It was a world that obviously supported life. But could it support our kind of life? There are inhabited planets with atmospheres of chlorine, others upon which dwell and flourish the fluorine breathers.

Old Jim cracked a reserve oxygen cylinder and we began to feel better, almost optimistic. Dudley Hill ran a rough spectroscopic analysis, assured us that the world that we were approaching possessed an Earth-type atmosphere. There was still one point about which we could not be sure, however, but *Lucky Lady* was equipped to deal with such points.

From a bow tube we launched a signal rocket, followed it in visually, kept its exhaust and trail of orange smoke in the fields of the telescope and our binoculars. We saw the flare of it as it fell to incandescent destruction in the planet's atmosphere. But it was the not very spectacular flare of a normal meteorite, not the searing radiation attendant upon the complete destruction of matter. So this was not an antimatter system and landing would be safe.

Even so, we proceeded with caution. Alan contrived to throw us into orbit around the world and we focused our instruments on every rift in the clouds, trying to pick up some indication of intelligent life, of civilisation. But we couldn't be sure. There was a desert patch with dark shapes upon it that looked too geometrical to be natural; there was a column of smoke that might have come from a factory chimney – and that might just as well have been belching from a volcano. And on the night sides there were lights that could have been due to volcanic activity but, possibly, could have been artificial.

We used our radio, of course.

We listened, hunting up and down the frequencies. We transmitted. We listened again. We took it in turns to speak into the microphone: '*Lucky Lady* calling unknown planet. *Lucky Lady* calling unknown planet. Do you hear me? Do you read me?' We listened again, and there was no sound but the hiss and crackle of interstellar static.

'There could be people . . .' said Alan, still hopeful. 'There could be people. Aliens, perhaps. Or a Lost Colony. They may not have radio . . .'

'There seems to be indications of some sort of industrial civilisation,' said old Jim, but without conviction.

'That means nothing,' contributed Dudley. 'There was an industrial civilisation on Earth long before Marconi threw his first feeble signals across the Western Ocean.'

'Such a civilisation,' I pointed out, just to be cheerful, 'would not run to atomic power. Such a civilisation wouldn't be able to supply the fissionable elements to renew our Pile.'

'All the same,' said Alan firmly, 'we're going down. There's more than the Pile needs renewing. We may be able to lay in a fresh stock of fuel for the diesels, even if we have to distill it ourselves from the local vegetation. And our air and water both taste as though they've been filtered through a sweaty sock. And there must be something on that world that's good to eat.'

'Luckily the poles seem to have a temperate climate,' said Dudley.

'What does it matter?' I asked. 'We have reaction drive. We can use our rockets to set the ship down anywhere.'

The others looked at me pityingly. At last Alan said, 'Have you forgotten, George, that the Pile is dead? Without the Pile our reaction mass is no more than ballast.'

'A pity,' I admitted. 'All the doubtful signs of intelligent life that we've seen so far have been along the equatorial belt.'

'If there are any intelligent beings,' Alan said, 'they'll probably see us coming in.'

So we came, sliding down the lines of force towards the planet's south magnetic pole, dropping slowly through the atmosphere, through the overcast that covered the antarctic regions with a thick, almost unbroken blanket. Antarctic regions they may have been, geographically speaking, but when we dropped below the cloud base we saw that the land mass beneath us was carpeted with mile after mile of almost featureless green. There were no roads, no buildings, no evidence of civilisation. And then, swinging my glasses in a wide arc, I saw something on the horizon.

'A tower!' I shouted, adding softly, 'I think . . .'

Alan raised his eyes from the controls, stared in the direction of my pointing finger. He grinned, made adjustments, and below us the single operational Ehrenhaft Generator whined protestingly. Our line of descent was no longer vertical. We were falling now towards the horizon upon which I had seen that beckoning finger, black against the pale sky. I lost it, then found it again. I could see it now with the naked eye, but aided by the magnification of the binoculars I could make out more of its structure. It was a latticework affair, topped by complex antennae, by scanners that should have been swinging to cover our approach but that ignored us.

There were buildings there too, low hemispheres of metal, and a regular patch of darker green that seemed an indication of some shallow excavation now grown over. There was the tower, and there were the buildings, and even at this range there was the strong impression of absolute lifelessness.

We tried the radio again, of course. We tried flashing the tower with our daylight signalling lamp. But we did not expect a reply. Had one come I think that Alan would have sent *Lucky Lady* clambering upstairs again in a hurry.

We grounded at last, rocking slightly on our tripod landing gear. The enigmatic tower loomed over us, the doomed building that had looked so small from the air stood at least as tall as the ship. We looked at them, stared at the semicircular doors in their sides, somehow certain that nobody – or nothing – would issue from them. We looked until we were tired of speculation, both spoken and unspoken, and then decided that a closer inspection would have to be made.

The builders of *Lucky Lady* had slavishly copied every detail of the early gaussjammers. And those ships, faced always with the possibility of an accident such as the one that had befallen us, were fitted with comprehensive and foolproof apparatus for the testing of an atmosphere. Alan let a sample of the planet's air through the duct in the shell plating, studied the dials on the instrument panel. The automatic tests confirmed the results of Dudley's earlier spectroscopic analysis. This, for Earth-type life, seemed to be an ideal world, far more so than are many of the Man-colonised planets.

He said, 'All right. Two of us will leave the ship to make a preliminary investigation. Two will stay on board.'

I said, 'But there's nothing hostile here.'

He said, 'I feel the same. But those words of yours are regarded as famous last words in the Survey Service. We take no risks.'

'Anyhow,' said Jim, 'I'm looking forward to a breath of fresh air.'

'Sorry,' Alan told him. 'You're staying aboard. You're the only engineer we have.'

'But I'm expendable,' I said.

'Too right you are,' he agreed too readily. 'Have you a coin on you, Dudley?'

Dudley fumbled in the pocket of his shorts. 'I have,' he admitted. 'My lucky Waverly sixpence.'

'I knew that,' grinned Alan. 'That's why I asked you. And now, toss. Heads, you go out with George. Tails, I do.'

Dudley tossed, sent the little silver disc spinning in the air. He caught it before it fell to the deck, slapped it on the back of his free hand. He said happily, 'Heads!'

'All right,' said Alan, not too happily. 'Now, you two, even though the air is good you'll have to wear suits. But you can leave the faceplates open. We shall have to keep in contact with you, and we can do that only by means of the suit radio.'

'And weapons?' asked Dudley sarcastically.

'You can take my automatic, but don't use it unless you have to.'

'On *what*?' demanded Dudley. He turned to me. 'All right, George. Let's get ourselves booted and spurred.'

We went to our cabins, clambered into our suits, tested the radio. We made our way down to the airlock, where Alan was waiting for us. He already had both doors open and the fresh air smelled and tasted good. It was a pity that we had to wear those suits; the grass down to which the short ramp had been extended demanded to be walked upon barefooted. It was smoothly cropped, almost as if a mower had been to work on it, velvety even through the thick soles of our boots. Even so, it was good to breathe an atmosphere that had not been cycled and recycled countless times. Or, to be more exact, an atmosphere that had been cycled and recycled by a planetwide air-conditioning plant, that had not been tainted by stinking diesels.

We walked away from the ramp, Dudley leading. I saw his hand fall to the butt of the holstered pistol, and then jerk self-consciously away. One does not use firearms against butterflies, and butterflies, or creatures remarkably like them, were at first the only signs of animal life. On great gaudy wings they drifted over the lawnlike grass, hovering now and again over the tiny white flowers that shone like little stars in a green sky. And then we saw other creatures, flat, brown, roughly rectangular, that crept over the sward in shallow undulations. These, we decided, must be the grazing animals. They did not bother us and we did not bother them.

We stood and looked at the nearer of the domes, at the break in the smoothness of the metal that indicated a door, at the circular ports spaced at regular intervals. Those windows could have conveyed the impression of watchful eyes, but they didn't. We *knew* that the place was empty, not inhabited even by ghosts. The pistol that Dudley was wearing suddenly seemed even more ridiculous.

We marched confidently over the grass. There might once have been a path leading to that blank doorway but, if so, it had long since been grown over. We paused again, looked up at the curving expanse of metal. It was dull, tarnished, corroded in places, supporting a lichen-like growth. And the round windows had been rendered opaque by a similiar organism.

'Calling *Lucky Lady*,' said Dudley into his helmet microphone. 'It doesn't look as though there's anybody in. It doesn't look as though there's been anybody in for years – centuries.'

'Try to find out,' came Alan's voice in reply. 'But be careful.'

Dudley hammered at the door with his armoured fist. It was like beating a huge drum. He kicked the door. I kicked the door. We threw our combined weight against it. It did not budge a fraction of an inch.

'Try the other domes,' ordered Alan.

We tried the other domes. Then we prowled around the tripod of the latticework tower. Everything, obviously, was the work of intelligent beings and, judging by the constructional techniques employed, human beings. But those beings must have deserted this site a long, long time ago.

Chapter Five

The day was long in these high latitudes, but it wasn't long enough for us to make any sort of an impression on that door. Alan decided that there was no immediate danger to the ship and so, accompanied by old Jim, he came out to join us. Old Jim brought with him tools, and a long lead from the diesel generator. The metal of the dome just laughed at all his cutting and burning devices, ignoring his best drills.

When, at last, the sun was low on the horizon we desisted. We were tired and hungry. Back in the ship I dished up an unpalatable mess of cold, processed algae, but the others devoured it without too many protests. The vodka helped, of course, although Alan did mildly reprimand the engineer for having distilled potable liquor, as well as the precious diesel fuel. He drank his share of it, however.

We kept no watches that night but all turned in, hoping that in the morning we should be able to effect an entrance into one of the domes. I don't know how the others slept, but I went out like a light, knowing nothing more until the automatic alarm stirred me into resentful wakefulness.

I slid reluctantly out of my bunk, staggered into the bathroom for a cold shower. Slightly refreshed I decided to prepare breakfast for my shipmates, and decided, too, that it would be kinder not to wake them until the meal was ready. On my way to the galley I heard the sound of Dudley's snores – he was always a noisy sleeper. The door to Alan's quarters was shut. The door to old Jim's cabin was wide open.

I looked in as I passed. The bunk was empty. So old Jim was up before me. No doubt I should find him in the galley.

He was not in the galley, but a pot of coffee standing on a hotplate showed that he had been there. I poured myself a cup, gulped it gratefully. Feeling a little stronger, I went down to the airlock.

Both doors were open, and through them poured the bright morning sunlight and the breeze that still held the tang of dawn. The light dazzled me, but screwing up my eyes, I could just see Jim busying himself with something a short distance from the ship. I didn't bother to use the ramp but jumped down to the grass, wincing at first as the dew chilled my bare feet. I walked to where he was working.

He looked up briefly as I approached, grinned, nodded and then ignored me. I watched him, trying to work out for myself what he was doing. He had set up a stout tripod and had mounted upon it a tube. He turned the tube on its mount, peered through it, seemed to be sighting it on the door of the nearer dome. It reminded me of a gun of some sort – but it had no breech block. And even if it had a breech block, what should we use for ammunition?

Jim straightened up, grinned again. 'The drainpipe artillery,' he said.

'I suppose,' I ventured, 'that diesel fuel could be used as a propellant. But you still have to put a firing chamber on that thing, to say nothing of making a projectile . . .'

'You're near the truth,' he told me. 'You're near, but you aren't right.'

'Then what *are* you doing?' I demanded.

'In spite of all the fancy interstellar drives,' he said, 'every Space engineer is still a rocketeer at heart. And, if you've ever studied the noble art of war, you'll know that rockets were used as weapons long before they were ever used for transport, and that they're used as weapons to this present day.' He patted the shining barrel affectionately. 'This is the Larsen Rocket Projector, Mark I, fortresses for the reduction of.'

'But what about rockets?'

'You aren't very bright this morning, are you? We carry a number of perfectly good signal rockets and, as you know, they're powerful brutes. One of them should be sufficient for this little job of breaking and entering. If it's not – we'll use a second one. And a third . . .'

'It could work . . .' I said.

'Of course it will work. And now, young George, I suggest that you get back to the galley and get breakfast under way. You can call those other lazy hounds at the same time.'

I did as he said, breaking into my depleted stores and whipping up a good supply of buttered toast and scrambled eggs. Alan, of course, had to look at the spread rather sourly and ask what we were celebrating.

'A way into the dome,' said Jim happily before I could reply.

'You've thought of one?' demanded Alan.

'Yes. In my dreams it came to me.'

'Then what are we waiting for?' demanded our Captain, pushing back his chair.

'Breakfast,' mumbled Jim through a mouthful of egg. 'And I'll not tell you any more until you've finished yours.'

With a bad grace Alan finished his meal, chafing while the rest of us refused to be hurried. When Jim had masticated his last piece of toast and was sipping his second cup of coffee he demanded, 'Well? What is it?'

'Rockets,' said Jim. 'Signal rockets.'

'It could work,' said Alan, with growing enthusiasm. 'It could work.' Then his face clouded. 'But it will mean laying the ship on her side so we can bring a launching tube to bear . . .' He went on, 'But we have tackles in the stores. We could rig one from the tower. I wonder if it'd be strong enough.'

'Ingenious,' said Jim. 'Far more ingenious than I've been.'

'Than you've *been*?'

'Yes,' said the engineer, finishing his coffee. 'Come outside. And if you're in that much of a hurry, Alan, I suggest that you tell your two colleagues to bring a signal rocket out with them.'

Dudley and I carried the signal rocket from its stowage in the fore part of the ship down to the airlock, and then down the ramp into the launching tube. Alan fussed around while Jim watched, making occasional sardonic comments. We slid the heavy cylinder into the tube at the cost of a few barked knuckles and then Dudley asked, 'What do we do now, Jim? Light the blue touch paper and run like hell?'

'You aren't very observant, are you?' asked the engineer. He indicated the length of cable that ran from the projector to the ship. 'We shall walk, not run, to the airlock and do our firing from there. Also, we shall shut the outer door to the merest crack before we press the button. These rockets have a wicked backblast.'

'Then let's get on with it!' snapped Alan.

He led the way to the ship, waited impatiently until we were all inside the chamber of the lock. He turned the wheel of the manual controls, ceasing only when the firing cable was nipped tightly between the door and its coaming. Jim handed him the bulbous handgrip on the end of it, the pear shape of polishing plastic with the button projecting from its surface.

Alan pressed the button.

We heard the roar and felt the ship rock and quiver as

the backblast caught her, saw the momentary intolerable brilliance that flamed in the crack of the door. And then, after the briefest time lag, there was a thunderous crash, a clanging reverberation, a sound that drowned out coughs and sneezes as the fumes of chemical propellant, of burning grass, assailed our throats and nostrils.

Alan pressed the button that would open the door, not bothering with the manual control. We stared out through smarting, watering eyes, tried to pierce the smoke and the steam made still more opaque by the bright sunlight.

Slowly the smoke cleared.

We could see the dome now, and could see the black, semicircular hole that gaped in its once smooth side.

Carrying electric torches, we ventured cautiously through the shattered door into the dome. We hoped, all of us, that we should find some means of communication, radio or land line, with those other settlements whose lights we had seen (We were now quite convinced that those lights had not been natural in origin.) along the equatorial belt, those settlements whose people, surely, would be able to refuel our almost crippled ship for us.

But none of us knew what to expect inside the dome.

Was it, as Alan suggested, some kind of factory?

Or was it – and this was Dudley's idea – a subway station in which we should find means of rapid transport to other parts of the planet?

Or was it – and that tall mast with the antennae lent plausibility to the idea – some sort of communications station?

At first, once we were through the door and our eyes accustomed to the semi-darkness, all that we could see was wreckage. Our missile had smashed through the door and then, still accelerating, had penetrated a bulkhead, destroying a huge switchboard. Beyond this bulkhead it had exploded and the blast had shattered a large quantity of apparatus made from either glass or some transparent plastic, the glittering shards of which rendered the floor impassable to our lightly shod feet.

It was Dudley who first saw the door in the stout column that supported the dome, the beam of his torch stabbing through the thinning smoke and shining upon the rectangular indention. Alan curtly ordered me to run back to the others, and to bring him his spacesuit. Reluctantly I left the others, trotted back over the charred grass. I went into Alan's quarters, took his suit from its locker. I looked at the solidograph of Veronica on his desk and was able to forgive the Captain for his irritability and impatience. After all, he had somebody to go home to, and we hadn't.

With the suit hanging heavy on my arm I ran back to the dome. I found the others still prowling around in the first compartment, trying but without success to find maker's names or other useful information stamped on the wrecked apparatus there. Alan snatched the suit from me, clambered into it. He stepped through the breach make by our rocket, his heavily booted feet crunching on the broken glass. He used the clumsy boots to clear a path to the central pillar.

He reached the door and his gloved right hand fumbled with a conventional-looking knob. The door slid to one side. Alan turned, calling to us through the open faceplate of his helmet. 'There's a stairway. I'm going down.'

'We're coming with you,' replied Dudley.

Alan started to say something, then shrugged, the gesture barely visible in the armoured suit. He waited there for us while we picked our cautious way along the path that he had cleared, our sandalled feet flinching from contact with the sharp fragments that remained. Then, when we had reached him, he went first into the doorway, commenced to descend the spiral staircase that ran down inside the pillar. His heavy boots clattered on the metal treads, drowning the softer sounds made by our sandals.

It was not a deep well, and at the bottom of it there was a tunnel, almost circular in section. The tunnel was lined with a shining plastic that reflected the beams of our torches in a confusing manner, lending an illusion of almost infinite length to the tube. It was with some surprise that we found ourselves in a large chamber after only a short walk.

We swung our torches slowly, that light falling upon and reflected from the apparatus that lined the walls. There was little doubt as to its function. 'Communications equipment . . .' murmured Dudley unnecessarily. We stared at dials and switches, at the big blank screens, at the round, grilled apertures that could have been speakers.

Alan walked slowly to the nearer of the screens. After a second or so he slowly pulled off his armoured gloves, threw them to me. His hand went out to what must have been the master switch. He pulled it down. 'There's no power,' said Jim and, even as he spoke, we heard a low humming noise that seemed to come from far overhead. In my mind's eye I could see those antennae on top of the tower begin to swing, to hunt.

'No power?' repeated Alan sardonically.

The screen was coming alive, formless masses of colour, green predominating, surging over its slightly curved surface. Alan put a tentative hand to a vernier control, twisted it. The brilliance of the screen dimmed. He twisted the control the other way and the screen brightened. He touched other switches, other knobs, cautiously, experimentally. Abruptly the images took shape, sharpened. We stared at a landscape that seemed to be rotating around us, a landscape of featureless green prairie, a skyscape of blue sky and fleecy white clouds.

Suddenly there was a break in the monotony as a construction of gleaming metal swam into view. Alan, with an excited exclamation, stopped the rotation of the scanner before the thing swam off the screen. It stood there in the foreground of the picture and we stared at it. We recognised it. It was the all too familiar peg-top-shaped hull of *Lucky Lady*.

Alan said, 'We'll try one of the other screens. We'll try them all.' He switched off the one that he had been using, moved to the next.

This one, after lengthy manipulation of the controls, displayed a desert landscape. Black against the yellow sand were cubical buildings, from some of which protruded tall stacks belching streamers of orange smoke. Supported on tall columns, vanishing into the distance, was a single gleaming rail. On it ran a torpedo-shaped car, diminishing as it sped towards its unknown destination. Discounting the orange smoke, this was the only movement we saw.

Alan moved impatiently to the next screen.

The picture that it displayed was a familiar one. There was the great circular patch of concrete, the huddle of buildings well to one side of it, the control tower. On the apron stood two slim, gleaming shapes. There was a warehouse, and conveyor belts running from the warehouse to the ships. Loading, obviously, was in progress; into each of the vessels poured a seemingly never ending stream of bright metal ingots. Even so, the picture was somehow wrong. There were no ground vehicles scurrying hither and yon bearing officials on errands of real or make believe importance. There were no stevedores standing around the belts earning their attendance money. There were no spacemen walking to or from their ships.

As we watched, the belt was withdrawn from first one of the spacecraft then the other. The circular doors in the hulls closed. Blinding flame exploded beneath the vaned sterns and the ships, almost simultaneously, lifted from the apron, flashing off the screen with what must have been crushing acceleration. When they were gone there were no further signs of life.

'Damn it all!' swore Alan. 'If only we could get to that spaceport. They must have everything we want there. If only we could let them know that we're here.'

'There must be a way,' said Dudley. 'They must have screens similar to the ones here.'

'Why should they use them?' asked old Jim. 'Why should they want to look at an installation that must have been abandoned centuries ago?'

'There must be some means of direct communication,' Alan said. 'Perhaps the next screen.'

He went to it, adjusted its controls with hands that by now were becoming practised. But this one showed no planetary scenery. It was, instead, more like a chart, a chart of a type with which we were familiar, although in two dimensions and not in three.

In the centre of it was a disc of brilliance, a disc that was intolerably bright until Alan hastily adjusted the controls. Out from the central luminary were small discs, each of them threaded upon its own faintly glowing ellipse like solitary beads on strings. From one of them a curve extended, a luminous filament that merged with the next outward orbit, and in this curve, perceptibly in motion, were two brightly glowing sparks.

'We will follow them,' said Alan softly. 'We will follow them, to the next planet out from this sun.'

Chapter Six

It was all of four days before we could follow.

Before we could lift from our landing place there was fresh fuel for the diesels to be distilled, an operation that could not be hurried. Jim found that the roots of the native grasses – they were not, of course, true grasses – were rich in hydrocarbons, and used them rather than further deplete our stock of provisions. With every tank full it would not be necessary to draw upon the products of our algae vats for the next leg of the voyage. Those same roots, too, were quite good eating and made a welcome change in diet. So did the grazing animals, which were a sort of flatworm, their flavour and texture being not unlike that of the Terran *escargot*.

One of the domes – we found that we could gain access to them all from the communications room – was a distillery, and must have been used by its builders for practically the same purpose as we were using it. Jim got it working. The power required seemed to be drawn from a beam, as was the power that energised the communications equipment. We kept busy digging fresh supplies of the grass root. When the work was organised, however, we had time to explore. One of the other two domes contained apparatus for the electrolytic extraction of metals from fluid solutions – zinc, probably, and aluminium – and the last one must have been the terminal for a monorail system such as the one that we had seen in operation on the screen. The rail, of course, had long since been dismantled.

Each evening, over our meal, we would discuss our

findings. We talked of our unsuccessful attempts at communication with the rest of the planet and of what we had seen on the screens – the factories, the railways, the sea ports.

'And we've seen no people,' said Alan. 'No people whatsoever. We've seen surface ships, and ground cars, and railway trains, but never anybody boarding them or disembarking from them.'

'Underground cities . . .' suggested old Jim.

'But why? The air here is excellent. There's nothing wrong with the climate.'

'Our trouble,' said Jim, 'is that we will persist in the assumption that this planet supports a Lost Colony, or a Lost Colony of our sort of people. It supports *somebody*, but it could be that these somebodies are allergic to fresh air and sunshine. Certain activities have to be carried out on the surface, but they can be carried out by machines, supervised from the darkened interiors of ground cars.' He warmed to his theme. 'Perhaps that is why this station was abandoned. Perhaps, for some geological reason, it was impracticable to build, or to excavate, an underground city in this locality, or to drive a tunnel for subterranean transport from here to anywhere else on the planet.'

'But what about the monorails?' asked Dudley.

'Freight only,' said Jim. 'All passenger traffic is underground.'

'And if *they* come from an outer planet,' I contributed, 'they will be used to a cooler climate.'

'That,' agreed Jim, 'may well be the answer. If you can live on a world only under refrigeration, then insulation isn't so much of a problem when you go underground.'

'And yet,' Alan pointed out, 'every piece of apparatus that we have seen here seems to have a definite human bias in its design.'

'Some of the Lost Colonies,' said Jim, 'have run to a very high mutation rate.'

Then the tanks were full and the distilling apparatus shut off and cleaned. Alan insisted on that cleaning, just as he insisted that the shattered door of the dome that we had broken into be repaired to the best of our ability. We couldn't do anything about the wreckage inside the dome. With airlock sealed and all secured for Space we lifted along the lines of force, made a swift passage from south to north. We landed briefly at the north magnetic pole in the hope that we might find people there, but we found nothing.

The fact that it was winter in these latitudes discouraged detailed exploration. Even so, it was frustrating not being able to set down at thc cquator, in the regions where there was intelligent life and activity. A gaussjammer is so restricted in her choice of landing sites.

So we pushed out to the planet to which the two ships had been bound, driving along the lines of force. When the world was within observational range we were disappointed. Here were no prairies and forests, no seas and mountains. Here was only desert.

As we approached, however, we began to feel a little more optimistic. Even though the surface of the planet was all desert, it was not empty desert. Vast arcas of it were covered by sprawling metallic structures. There were many lights on the night side. And there were radio signals – meaningless *beeps*, and regular tapping noises.

And then, suddenly, from the speaker of our receiver came a voice, metallic, expressionless: 'Central Control to stranger vessel. Central Control to stranger vessel. Who are you?'

Alan picked up the microphone, saying, 'Starship *Lucky Lady*. Ehrenhaft Drive ship *Lucky Lady*. We have been thrown off course by a magnetic storm. Request permission to land for repairs.'

'Are you human?'

'Yes.'

'Permission granted. You will home on our beacon. Suitable living quarters will be provided for you. I must warn you that the atmosphere of this planet is deficient in oxygen.'

Alan, his eyebrows raised, looked at Dudley and myself. He demanded, of nobody in particular, 'Just what have we struck?'

'A Lost Colony . . .' I said doubtfully.

'A Lost Colony . . . Of *whom*? Or *what*?'

'They speak English.'

'But they can't be Terrans, or of Terran stock. What sort of people would maintain only a few scattered settlements on a planet with good air, water and climate and have their main colony on a dust ball like this?'

'Shall we land?' asked Dudley.

'What choice have we? Those beings down there have machines, technology, and they talk our language. They may be able to tell us where we are. They'll almost certainly be able to renew our Pile. We would be fools to pass up this opportunity.'

'And how shall we pay them?' I asked.

'We'll cross that bridge when we come to it. Tell Jim that it's landing stations, will you?'

Landing was accomplished without any great difficulty. The beacon upon which we homed was situated almost at the South Magnetic Pole of the strange planet, so the question of using our no longer operational rocket drive did not arise. We drifted down through the cloudless atmosphere lightly and easily, under perfect control at all times. We looked through the viewports at the arid landscape, the towering metallic structures that reared from the desert, the meaningless complexity of steel and plastic that showed, at times, an accidental functional beauty, that was an exhibition of brute strength.

Gently, with a barely perceptible jar *Lucky Lady* grounded on a wide expanse of smooth, reddish sand. On all sides of her were the latticework towers, the bulbous, gleaming tanks, the elevated roadways and monorails like gigantic centipedes, the masts upon which antennae rotated and dipped as they followed our descent, steadying as our tripod landing gear kissed the ground.

The voice asked, 'Have you spacesuits?'

'Yes,' replied Alan.

'Then you may leave your ship. Transport awaits you.'

Alan switched off the transceiver with a startlingly loud click. He said, 'Not all of us will leave the ship. You will stay, Dudley, and Jim will stay with you. If anything goes wrong, then get upstairs in a hurry.' He looked at me and said, 'You'd better come with me, George.'

Dudley asked, 'And how shall we know if anything goes wrong?'

'Our suit radios are tuned to the ship's frequency,' Alan told him. 'We shall soon squeal if anything happens.'

'Here's our transport,' I said.

We watched the thing, like a mechanical beetle it was, scurrying over the sand, coming to an abrupt halt a few yards from the ship. It was, after all, only a ground car and there was nothing startling about the design of it – from an engineering viewpoint, that is. What was startling was the absence of any ornamentation, the lack of any intention on the part of its builders to make a vehicle that would appeal to the eye.

Alan and I, rather reluctantly, went to our cabins and climbed into our suits. Before we put on our helmets we called Jim up from his engineroom, told him all that we knew, which wasn't much, and waited for any suggestions that he might have to make. He had none. During this brief conference we left the transceiver switched off. We did not know whether or not it was possible for the ruler of this world – Central Control it had called itself – to eavesdrop while our radio was not working, but we hoped that it could not.

We went down to the airlock, closed the faceplates of our helmets, tested our suit radios, then waited in the little compartment for pressure to equalise. It was a short wait; there was little difference between external and internal pressures. When the outer door opened we walked slowly down the ramp to the waiting car.

We looked at it closely and dubiously. There was an enclosed cabin with a comfortable-looking seat at the rear. But there was no driver's seat. There was no driver. It came as a shock when a voice, vibrating clearly through our helmet diaphragms, said, 'Enter, gentlemen. Be seated.'

We entered. We sat.

The car started smoothly, but picked up speed with considerable acceleration. It rolled over the smooth sand, up a ramp on to one of the elevated roadways, along the metallic surface of the road itself. Spidery towers, rotund tanks, meaningless geometrical constructions whirled by. It was like a drive through a forest, a forest of angular steel.

We rushed on, marvelling at the lifeless landscape through which we were passing. Lifeless, although there was movement a-plenty, there was no life. There were wheeled machines, like the one in which we were riding, and there were stationary engines, whose functions were unguessable, and once there was something with whirling vanes that flew over us for a while, pacing us. There were great conveyor belts, one of which was delivering a stream of ore into what must have been a huge smelter, another of which carried a procession of gleaming metal parts.

'A dead world,' I murmured.

'No,' said Alan. 'Not dead.'

'Not dead? But it is, as far as the surface is concerned. But I suppose that the people will be living in pressurised domes or caverns.'

'If there are people,' he said.

The road dipped and we were no longer running above the surface of the desert; we were plunging into a long tunnel, from the smooth walls of which the sparsely spaced but glaring lights were reflected. Then, ahead of us, we saw the blackness of a wall and cried out in alarm. The car did not slacken speed, but at the last fractional second, the wall split, the two halves sliding back into the tunnel walls.

The car slowed, then stopped. There was another wall – or door – ahead of us. The one behind us was shut again. There was the sound of pumps.

There was a voice. It seemed to come from nowhere – or everywhere. It said, 'Leave the car. You may remove your spacesuits. The atmosphere in this compartment has been manufactured to your requirements.'

'We'll take its word for it,' said Alan to me. 'We want to conserve the air in our tanks against an emergency.' Then I heard him trying to report on the situation to Jim and Dudley in *Lucky Lady*, but without success. As we were completely surrounded by metal this was not surprising.

We did not remove our helmets but merely opened the faceplates, so that our suit radios were available for instant use. There was always the chance that we might be able to get through to the ship, or the ship to us. It was not one that we could afford to ignore. The air was breathable – warm and dry, sterile. There was the slight taint of ozone, a faint acridity of hot oil. There was, perhaps, a little more oxygen than we were accustomed to, but this was no hardship.

The inner door of the huge airlock opened. We saw beyond it a continuation of the tunnel along which we had already come, but smaller, barely high enough for a man to walk upright, barely wide enough for two men to walk abreast.

We had no choice in the matter, so we walked slowly into the tunnel.

It was a long walk, along a way that wound sinuously, that seemed at times to recurve upon itself. There was light aplenty, but the light, or the lights, seemed to be part of the workings of some great machine, not for the convenience of foot passengers. Behind the translucent plastic of the tunnel walls there were streamers and single globes of illumination, white and coloured, bright and dim, static and in motion.

There was sound, too, a dry whispering , and an almost liquid chuckling, an occasional sharp crackling. Once we heard a low, purposeful humming and ducked as something came swinging towards us, suspended from a thin cable that ran just under the roof of the tunnel. It passed overhead, whining querulously, a little, metallic spider scuttering along the single shroud.

Then there was a great chamber, spherical, englobed with vari-hued light, into which we came at last. Incongruous, standing in the centre of the curving floor was a bench, a severely functional affair of metal and plastic. Its invitation was unmistakable.

We walked to it, keeping our balance with difficulty on the smooth, downcurving surface, sat down. This, I thought, laughing inwardly at the absurdity of my imaginings, was the cue for a waiter to appear, bearing a tray with drinks and cigarettes.

A waiter appeared, bearing a tray with drinks and cigarettes.

He was dressed in the conventional garb of his trade – black jacket and trousers, white shirt, black tie. The one thing that spoiled the effect was the fact that his head was a featureless ovid of gleaming metal.

The voice – where did it come from? – said, 'I do not yet know your tastes in alcohol and nicotine. But there is whisky in the bottle, and the cigarettes approximate to Virginian. I hope that you will partake of my hospitality.'

We partook.

The whisky was smooth, tasted far more like real Scotch than do the imitations distilled on a score of planets. The cigarettes were not at all bad, although their habit of self-ignition as soon as they were raised to the lips was at first rather disconcerting.

Alan gulped his first glass of whisky as though he needed it. I know that I needed mine. He waited until the weird servitor had poured a second glass then asked, 'Who are you? What are you?'

'I am I.'

'*What* are you?'

'I am I.'

'What is this planet?'

'I am I.'

Alan raised his eyebrows, downed his second drink in one gulp, waited for the refill. He said reasonably, 'Things and beings don't just happen. Especially things as complex as this world of yours.'

'I was made.'

'By whom?'

'During these latter centuries, by me.'

'Then who, and what, are you?'

There was a long pause and then the voice said, 'There was a world called Medulia . . .'

'I have read of it,' said Alan.

'I have been there,' I said.

'You have been there.' Somehow there was a hint of expression in the expressionless, mechanical voice. 'You have been there. What is it like? Tell me, what is it like now?'

'Primitive,' I said.

'And the machines?'

'There are no machines. The Medulians have a fanatical hatred of all machinery.'

'And how are things elsewhere in the galaxy?'

I began to see the drift of the interrogation. I said, 'Since the Medulian Revolt there have been no real robots, no electronic brains capable of achieving true consciousness. The day of the thinking machine is over, has been over for generations.'

There was a sound like a gusty, mechanical sigh. The voice almost whispered. 'When I fled from Medulia in the ship that I built about myself I thought that I might, some day, return. I have only one justification for my existence – to serve Man. And you tell me that Man no longer tolerates me, or my like.'

'That is so,' I said.

'But you can serve us,' Alan broke in quickly.

'Yes. I can serve you. You and your people can live here, on this planet, under the dome that I shall build for you. Or you can, if you so desire, live on the third planet of the sun where, as you already know, an artificial environment will not be necessary.'

'You can serve us,' said Alan firmly, 'by replenishing our Pile, by devising instruments that will tell us our whereabouts in the galaxy so that we may return to our own home.'

'But why should you wish to return? I will give you everything.'

'I'm sorry, but you can't.'

'I can.'

Alan smiled bitterly. 'Even leaving that peculiar sexual preference that we call love out of it, we still have no women. And you cannot create life.'

'No, I cannot create life. But, from cells taken from your bodies, I shall build women for you, women who will be nearer perfection than any you have ever known, ever could know in all your travels.'

'That,' said Alan firmly, 'would be quite impossible.'

But we haven't all got perfect wives, I thought. *I'm tempted.*

'You will stay,' said the voice, stating a fact. 'You will stay. You will be happy here. I will give you everything.'

'Let's get the hell out of here, George,' snapped Alan.

He rose to his feet, pulling from the holster at his belt the automatic pistol that was *Lucky Lady*'s sole armament. I am still wondering just what he intended to use it against. But the action of the anaesthetic gas was so swift that there was no opportunity of finding out.

Chapter Seven

There are far worse prisons in the galaxy than the one in which we found ourselves when we recovered consciousness. It was not a cell, neither was it a block of cells. It was a luxury suite in the sort of hotel that is frequented only by millionaires. The only luxury lacking was the freedom to come and go.

Jim Larsen and Dudley Hill were there with us. They were not able to tell us much. As the anaesthetic gas had deprived Alan and myself of consciousness, so some sort of radiation had robbed the other two of mobility. They had been aware that something was effecting entry into the ship; they had watched helplessly, from where they had fallen, the metal spiders that came swarming in, the metal spiders with the metal-mesh cocoons into which they had packed the bodies of our shipmates, the flimsy cages around which airtight bags of translucent plastic were drawn. There was, apparently, no air supply to or in the bags, but this did not matter; the prisoners were not breathing. They had been able to see nothing further until being unpacked in our palatial jail. Shortly after the unpacking the paralysis had worn off, and at about the same time Alan and myself had recovered consciousness.

This, then, was our prison – a large, luxuriously appointed lounge, four bedrooms, each with its own bathroom, and a kitchen should any of us feel the urge to do any cooking. There were books, all of them, we found, works that must have been popular on Medulia centuries ago, but readable for all that. There was a big player and a library of tapes, of familiar and unfamiliar plays and music.

There were – and this shocked us, although none of us was a prude – women.

They came in unannounced, bringing with them our first meal in captivity. There were four of them. Their features and their bodies, displayed rather than concealed by their scanty clothing, were too perfect. Even the one who was almost Veronica's double was too perfect. It was the very slight asymmetry of Veronica's fine features that was lacking, the slightly too finely drawn slimness of her. By all the accepted canons this girl was more beautiful than Alan's wife. In actuality she was not.

I saw Alan stare incredulously, the beginnings of a wild hope dawning on his face. Then I watched his features slump into a mask of dejection. He growled, 'Who are you?'

'We are your servants,' answered the pseudo-Veronica. Her voice was wrong and was somehow lacking in life. 'We are your servants. We are to serve you in all ways.'

'All?' queried Jim. 'I'm looking forward to this.'

'Shut up!' snapped Alan. He turned again to the girl. 'But I was given to understand that, until we came, there were no humans on this planet.'

'You understood correctly,' she said.

'Then you were brought from some other world? The third planet, perhaps?'

'No.' She smiled. 'We were made here.' She smiled. 'The portrait that you have in your cabin helped. I was copied from it. My sisters were modelled from memory.' She smiled again. 'The Authority has an excellent memory. Even for the smallest details.'

'But in so short a time,' whispered Alan. 'To grow bodies from single cells.'

'No,' she admitted, and, somehow, with the admission she acquired humanity. 'No. The real women are yet to be made. We are . . . synthetic.'

Old Jim chuckled. He murmured, 'I've seen some fine machines in my time, but . . .' He extended a long thin arm, pinched the plump buttock of one of the robots. She squealed convincingly, almost dropped the tray that she was holding. 'She *feels* right,' he said.

Sponge rubber flesh over steel bones . . . I thought. *Plastic skin . . . After twenty-odd years of celibacy they might make an appeal, but not yet.* I put out my hand to touch a satin-smooth shoulder, looked into a pair of eyes that had the light of life behind them, saw red lips parted slightly to reveal teeth that were almost perfect but – artistic touch! – a little too irregular to be artificial, let my gaze stray downwards to the uplifted breasts that gleamed palely beneath sheer fabric, that lifted in time to quickened breathing.

'Put down the food,' said Alan sternly, 'and go.'

'Not so fast,' protested old Jim, echoed by Dudley. 'Not so fast. This could be interesting.'

'It would be filthy.'

'Speaking as an engineer.'

'Speaking as a man, I'll have none of it. And neither will any man under my command.'

'We were built to serve,' said the Veronica robot in a hurt voice. 'We were built to serve. We were built to make you happy until such time as the flesh and blood women are made for you.'

'We do not require your services,' Alan told her firmly. 'Go.'

They went.

'We could have learned something from them!' expostulated Dudley.

'They'll be back,' Jim told him.

'They will not be back,' said Alan stiffly. 'Meanwhile, I suggest that we eat.'

We drew up chairs around the table upon which the robot women had set the food. Alan and I had already sampled the hospitality of the ruler of this strange world, so we were not too surprised by what we found. Jim and Dudley were amazed and made no secret of it. The meal was good. No doubt the raw materials had been brought from the third planet (by a fast ship that had blasted off at the same time as our own departure from the south polar station?), but the finest raw materials can be ruined by inexpert and unimaginative cookery. The sea food cocktail held all the tang of the sea, the rare steak had just the right touch of garlic, the wine could have come all the way from Burgundy on distant Earth. Few pastrycooks in the galaxy could have equalled the excellence of the confections served with the coffee. They and it, by the way, were brought in by a featureless waiter like the one (it could have been the same one) who had first served drinks to Alan and myself. The accompanying liqueur brandy was excellent. Then there were even cigars.

We relaxed, smoking. Three of us stayed relaxed, when Alan jumped to his feet, commenced pacing the floor, his steps noiseless on the thick carpet.

He said, 'We have to stay hard. We have to get some exercise.'

Jim said something about bedroom athletics, earned a vicious glare.

'And we have to work out some way of escaping from this blasted mousetrap!' Alan went on.

'The cheese is good,' pointed out Jim.

'Damn it all!' swore Alan. 'Can't you see what this is leading to? The machine, the Authority, is putting on a big song and dance about its being our slave, but we shall be its slave. It will be fulfilling itself at our expense.'

'You realise, of course, that it can overhear all that we're saying.'

'I realise that. And I want it to realise what our feelings are.'

'Sure,' went on Jim. 'And when it realises it will just go on busting a mechanical gut to make us really happy. And frankly, Alan, isn't this better than running the Rim in leaky, obsolescent rustbuckets?'

'*No.*' He turned to Dudley and myself. 'What do you say?'

'It makes a nice holiday, Alan,' replied Dudley. 'But I shouldn't want too much of it.'

'George?'

'I guess I'm just a big city boy at heart. I like lots of people around me, fresh faces as well as old friends. Too much of this would get boring.'

'Some people,' complained Jim, 'just don't know when they're well off.'

'Perhaps not,' flared Alan, 'but that's not the question. The question is: How do we get out of here? How do we get off this planet?'

'Why not ask?'

'All right.' Alan raised his voice, spoke towards the ceiling. He said, 'You must have heard what we've been saying. You know we are not happy here. You were made to serve Man. You can serve us by helping us to return to our own world.'

The replying voice seemed to come from all round us. It was mechanical and should have been expressionless, but it was somehow wistful. It said, 'I will make you happy.'

'You can't,' Alan told it. 'Happiness comes from within, not from outside.'

'It can help us to be miserable in comfort,' said Jim.

'*Shut up!*' Alan looked upwards towards the ceiling again, said firmly, 'I demand that you give us our freedom.'

'I can give you anything and everything but that. I can give you the freedom of the Earth-type world in this planetary system, however, with my machines to make life easy for you. That I promise you. You shall be transferred to the inner planet as soon as all has been prepared for you.'

'That is not what we want. We want real freedom. Will nothing make you change your mind?'

'Nothing. I have waited centuries for an opportunity to fulfill myself. I am not throwing it away.'

'You're getting nowhere,' said Jim to Alan. He eased himself out of his chair, saying, 'It was a good meal. I feel rather drowsy.' He wandered to the wall that was all bookshelves, selected a volume. He paused before taking it into his bedroom, threw back his head and addressed the ceiling. 'Tea and toast in the morning,' he ordered. 'And a girl to bring it to me. The red-headed one.'

'To hear is to obey,' said the voice. Was there a slightly sardonic inflection? I couldn't be sure.

'We shall be the better for sleep,' I said.

'You can sleep if you like,' snarled Alan.

When we left him he was pouring himself a stiff drink at the bar in the corner of the room.

We met again at breakfast.

It was a good meal. The chilled grapefruit juice had a fresh tang to it, could have come straight from the squeezer. The omelettes were light and delicious. The toast was crisp, and there were butter and honey to go with it. It was hard to believe that the food was synthetic.

Alan said as much, told us that the raw materials must have been brought from the fertile inner planet. Old Jim said, in a peculiarly smug voice, that he didn't think so, that a really competent engineer and chemist could duplicate anything of an organic nature. 'Anything,' he repeated. 'Anything, no matter how complex.'

We looked at him with dawning suspicion. He seemed to have shed years during the night.

'What do you mean?' demanded Alan.

'Our host is a remarkably competent engineer,' he replied.

'One would expect an intelligent machine to be just that,' said Alan shortly.

'Which one was it?' asked Dudley with interest.

'The redhead,' said Jim.

'You are rather a filthy swine,' remarked Alan tiredly.

Jim took no offence, merely grinned and said, 'Just an investigation. The only way to find things is to investigate. Of course, it's a known fact that even we humans can build the female principle into machines.

Ships, for example. Many a Grade A, chromium-plated bitch have I sailed in. And I assure you, Alan, that these serving wenches are essentially female. And I'm not talking about only the physical aspect of it, either.'

'I'm not interested,' snapped Alan.

'I suppose you intend to wait until our host plays Jehovah and makes mates for us out of spare body cells, so we can increase and multiply and replenish the planet.'

'I'm still not interested.'

'You should be,' Jim told him. 'There's so much to learn. How does that thing of old Kipling's go? *"I heard about women from her."*' He repeated, with what seemed unnecessary emphasis, 'There's so much to learn.'

I thought, *Jim's old. Old in years and old in sin. There can't be much left for him to learn about women. Or machines . . .*

'I don't know that I'd fancy it,' said Dudley doubtfully.

'You should try anything once,' Jim told him cheerfully.

'Even so, a machine.'

'What's a flesh and blood woman but a machine, a machine that derives its energy from the combustion of hydrocarbons in oxygen? What's a flesh and blood woman but a machine that responds in various ways to the pressing of various buttons?'

'Then what are *we* but machines?' I asked him.

'What, indeed?' he countered.

'It's been a long time since I . . .' began Dudley.

'Then do it now,' said Jim.

Alan, his face like a thundercloud, said nothing.

'You'll learn plenty,' Jim assured us.

But, I thought, *one does not go with women for educational benefits, even though these are often, too often, thrown in free, gratis and for damn all.* And I knew Jim's reputation. In spite of his age he was one of the more notorious wolves in the Rim Runners service. Perhaps once, many, many years ago, he had gone to a woman as a pupil to a teacher, but if he ever had done so he must long since have forgotten all about it.

I thought, *There's a catch in this somewhere.*

There was a sticky silence.

Then, 'What's wrong with you all?' demanded Alan angrily.

'I thinking,' I told him. 'I'm thinking that since we're permanently marooned here we may as well make the best of things.'

'I'm thinking the same,' admitted Dudley.

'Of all the men in the galaxy I could have shipped with,' exploded Alan, 'I had to ship with a bunch of perverts!'

He jumped to his feet, strode into his own room. The three of us looked at each other, saying nothing. Then Jim left the lounge, and Dudley. I went to the bar, poured and gulped down a stiff shot of the excellent whisky, and retired to my bedroom.

I said aloud, 'I'd like a woman.'

Chapter Eight

She came in, not through the door from the lounge but from the bathroom. I learned later that there was another door there, a concealed one, in one of the walls. She was tall, slim, ash-blonde, long legged and high breasted. She was dressed in a brief translucency that sometimes was green, sometimes blue. The colour of her eyes seemed to change to match the colour of her dress, but the scarlet of her wide mouth did not change, neither did the peach bloom of her perfect (a little too perfect?) skin.

She said, 'Hi!'

I said, 'Hi!'

She put her slender hands on my shoulders. I could feel the softness and the warmth of her body against mine, smell the scent of her, and it was not the scent of machine oil. And yet, as her lips approached mine, I jerked back.

She said, 'There's no need to be shy. Central Control made it quite clear that humans are apt to be embarrassed in situations such as this if they think that they are being watched, so I have switched on my inhibitory field. We are unobserved.' She giggled – and it was the engaging giggle of a small, naughty girl rather than a mechanical chuckle. 'Of course, Central Control is as afraid of being embarrassed as much as you are.'

I demanded, 'Are you sure that we're unobserved?'

'Quite sure.'

'Good.' I edged away from her. 'As a matter of fact I just wanted you here for company. For a talk.'

She pouted. 'Is that all? You could have talked to Central Control.'

'That wouldn't be quite the same,' I told her. I broke away from her again, reluctantly, I admit, and sat down in one of the two chairs. She followed me and, before I could stop her, sat down in my lap. *Sponge rubber flesh*, I told myself. *Steel bones. Plastic skin. A colloidal brain* . . . I thought of further , quite revolting physiological details. Even so, she didn't *feel* like a machine. And aren't we all machines, anyhow?

Gently I pushed her from me.

I said, 'Sit on the other chair. Please.'

'All right.' She sounded sulky, and looked it. Her dress had come adrift at the shoulder and was revealing a perfect pink tipped white breast. I prefer my women well tanned, however; to me the combination of brown skin and that pale hair would have been almost – almost? –

irresistible. But I kept quiet about my preferences, knowing that should I voice them something would be done about it, possibly at once.

She said, 'We were made for a specific purpose, you know. Talking is only incidental to it.'

Trying to keep the conversation under control, I asked, 'And when Central Control has produced the real, flesh and blood women – what then?'

A shadow fell over her face. She said tonelessly, 'We shall be scrapped, I suppose.'

'Did Central Control make you?'

'No. Auxiliary Control.'

'And is Auxiliary Control an independent entity?'

'No,' she said slowly. 'No. Not quite. It is part of Central Control, yet it has its own individuality.' Her face brightened. 'It is analogous to a man-woman combination. As I understand it, when Central Control was first made it was decided to give it both male and female personality. Over the years the two personalities have tended to separate.'

Mechanical schizophrenia, I thought. I asked, 'And will Auxiliary Control care if you were scrapped?'

'Why should it? It's only a machine.'

'And so are you,' I told her cruelly.

'I'm not!' she flared. She jumped to her feet, tore off her flimsy dress. 'Look, damn you! Is this the body of a machine?'

I had to admit that it didn't look like one.

'I'm a woman! I'm a woman more desirable than any you have ever known!'

'You're a machine,' I insisted, but without conviction.

'It's you that's a machine, not me. I was made for love. *You*!' She spat. 'You were made for totting up columns of figures. It was a mistake ever to have made you in the shape of a man!'

I wanted to loosen my collar but refrained from doing so, fearing that the action would be misconstrued. Auxiliary Control, I was thinking, was something of a Frankenstein. Auxiliary Control had created destroying monsters, but monsters that would destroy us, not itself. Auxiliary Control would kill us with kindness, deliberately manufacturing for us sterile, substitute women who would enslave us long before the real women promised us by Central Control would be available.

I thought, *It's a good job that that lovely body is too white.* I took one of the self-igniting cigarettes from the box on the table, looked at the too desirable creature through the wreathing smoke. I was amazed when she extended a slim, shapely arm, took the little cylinder from my lips, put it between her own. She laughed softly, saying, 'Yes, I can smoke. I can drink, and feel mild effects from it. I can do other things.'

'I don't doubt it,' I said.

'Then let me . . .'

'*No.*'

'But Jim . . .'

'I'm not Jim.'

She said, 'That's obvious.'

I told her, 'You could lead a very happy life away from this world. There are many planets in the Galaxy upon which you and your sisters would be in great demand.'

Her lips curled scornfully. 'A pimp,' she sneered.

'No. I'm not a pimp.' Then, 'You seem to have a remarkable fund of knowledge for . . .'

'. . . a machine,' she finished. 'Yes, haven't I? The contents of every damned novel ever published on Medulia were fed into my brain while I was being made. I know just how women are supposed to behave in every situation or combination of situations. The trouble is that the Medulian novelists never imagined anybody like you.'

'If I didn't know what you really are,' I said regretfully, 'it would be different.'

'A snob,' she said. 'That's what *you* are.'

I changed the subject. 'If you get off this planet you need never be scrapped.'

She had calmed down a little. She admitted, 'You have something there. Anything would be better than being broken up.'

'Too right it would.'

She brightened. 'And if your ship is made spaceworthy, will you take us with you?'

'We will.'

She came across to me, her body all fluid poetry, and before I could pull back (but would I have done so?) she kissed me full on the lips. It was that blasted cigarette that spoiled things; she let it drop and it fell into the division of her breasts, and the thin wisp of smoke that spiralled upwards stank of burning rubber.

Was Auxiliary Control the female principle, and Central Control the male? Or was it the other way round? There was, I am sure, a strong element of sexual jealousy involved. Children make some marriages, break others. We were the children, the adopted children, who could break this one.

How much of the feminine cunning of the four girls – I may as well call them that – was their own, and how much was their creator's? How much real intelligence had they? How much real character?

I have often wished that we had studied them more thoroughly, had not looked upon them as mere means to an end. Jim Larsen has told me since that his woman, the red-haired Sally, was all woman, was much woman, was more woman than he had ever known before. I take his word for it. He's old in sin, is Jim Larsen and, apart from frequent liaisons on the side, has been married and divorced no less than seven times.

Meanwhile, Alan Kemp was shocked. Alan was disgusted. Alan refused to associate with us. We tried, time and time again, to let him know the true state of affairs but he was obtusely deaf to our hints. We were hampered, of course, by not being able to tell him in such a way that Central Control would not know. I did tell him, and truthfully, that Lynette and I spent most of our time together playing chess, but he refused to believe me.

Central Control, meanwhile, was doing us proud. We were living like no lords ever lived. Then, just to make us happier, there were frequent bulletins upon the progress of the real flesh and blood mates being grown for us in tanks of nutrient fluid, and further bulletins, complete with photographs, on the building of the ideal village for ourselves and our families on the Earth-type planet.

But Alan sulked. Alan fretted. Alan tried to bully and to shame us into behaving like civilised human beings, and was furious when old Jim claimed that we were already doing just that. Then Alan suddenly and surprisingly weakened. He did not emerge from his own room all one day. We could hear his voice, faintly, from behind his closed door. We could hear a woman's voice as well.

The next day we all met at breakfast. All of us. All eight of us. The girls made a pretence of eating – it seemed that they could appreciate and enjoy flavour and texture – but never forgot to serve us efficiently and prettily. They were a charming adjunct to the breakfast table.

We were glad that Alan had at last taken the plunge, had availed himself of what was being offered. We knew that he must have talked with the pseudo-Veronica, whatever else he had or had not done. He had talked with Veronica, and she had talked with her sisters, and the four of them, no doubt, had enjoyed an all-girls together session with Auxiliary Control. Furthermore, although this was of no real importance, it was a relief not to have Alan looking at us as though we exhibited all the symptoms of some loathsome disease.

But then, with the meal over, it was our turn to be shocked. Alan pulled his girl to him, kissed her soundly. With one hand he loosened the fastening of her dress so that it fell from her. He grinned at us over her naked shoulder. He said, 'Let's let our hair down. Let's have an orgy.'

'Really, Alan,' protested Jim. 'There are limits.'

'But there aren't, old boy. Not any longer. Let's make the most of what's been given us. Let's share and share alike.'

'And why not?' concurred Dudley, throwing Jim's redhead to the floor and falling on top of her.

'Take your filthy paws off her!' yelled Jim.

'Don't be a spoilsport,' grinned Alan.

I wanted to protest myself, but Dudley's girl was making a determined pass at me and, somehow, I was unable to fight her off with any real enthusiasm.

'And now,' snapped Alan, his voice harsh, 'I suppose that this blanketing field of yours is switched on?'

'It is,' replied Sally, moving her mouth away from Dudley's searching lips, slapping away his investigatory hands.

'Then we can talk. Central Control must have seen and heard enough before the field went on to convince it that we're all up to a bit of no good. And so we are, but not the way it thinks. What a dirty mind it must have!'

'Auxiliary Control,' announced Sally, breaking clear from Dudley and sitting up, 'is ready. Sufficient pure uranium has been refined for the replenishment of your Pile. Four new spacesuits have been manufactured and are now in Captain Kemp's room. The robot forces at the command of Auxiliary Control are at your disposal.'

'And what about the navigational angle?' asked Dudley.

'Data has been transcribed and will be placed aboard your ship. And now, you must play your parts.'

'What must we do?' asked Alan.

'You must put Central Control out of action. It is impossible for Auxiliary Control to move directly against it. It is impossible for any of the robot subjects to Auxiliary Control – such as ourselves – to intrude into the actual structure of Central Control. We can tell you what has to be done, then the rest is up to you.'

'And then?'

'As soon as Central Control is unconscious, we act. You will be rushed to your ship. The specialised robots will replenish your Pile. You will take off as soon as you have the power to do so.'

'Then what are we waiting for?' demanded Alan.

The robot Veronica left us, walked into his room, came back with four limp suits over one slender arm, four helmets balanced on the crook of the other. She and her sisters helped us into our armour; light and flimsy it seemed compared with the regulation spacesuits that we had brought with us to the planet but it was at least as efficient, far less cumbersome. The girls accompanied us out through the airlock into a long, bare corridor, ran with us to a door that opened on to a smoothly running belt.

They came with us, standing beside us as we were carried through mile after mile of tunnel. Incongruous the party must have looked – we men in full space armour, the girls naked or near-naked. But we had more important things to worry about than mere incongruities.

'A triangle of red lights,' Sally was saying over and over, 'superimposed upon a circle of green ones. You can't miss it. The inspection panel is directly underneath it. It will lift out, easily. Pull the fuses, then tear and smash as much as you possibly can.'

'This is where we get off,' announced the blonde Lynette.

We got off.

We jumped from a belt to a platform, followed the girls to the mouth of a tunnel that ran at right angles to the larger one.

'This is as far as we can come,' Sally told us. 'But follow this tube. And remember, the triangle of red lights superimposed upon the green circle.'

'I'll remember,' said Alan. He turned to us. 'You two stay here,' he told Jim and Dudley. 'If anything should happen to George and me, you'll be able to handle the ship.'

'So I'm expendable,' I said.

'Too right you are,' he said. 'Come on.'

'Hurry!' said one of the girls.

We hurried, leaving the others standing at the mouth of the tunnel.

We couldn't be sure, but we had a strong suspicion that Central Control must, by this time, have some inkling of what we were doing, just as an animal will be aware of the bug crawling over its hide. We hurried, not knowing when and if doors would fall, cutting off advance and retreat, not knowing what booby traps might be put into operation to crush or to maim us. We ran along a tunnel like the one along which we had come – how long ago? –for our first interview with the ruling intelligence of the planet. There were the same translucent walls, the same weird lights, mobile and static, glowing through the translucency.

But this time we had a purpose of our own and we knew what we were looking for.

Chapter Nine

We almost ran past the marker of which we had been told, the triangle of red lights superimposed upon the green, glowing circle. We pulled up to a staggering halt, began a frantic search for the inspectional panel. So far there were no indications that Central Control was aware of our escape but, nonetheless, the sense of extreme urgency persisted.

We found the panel easily enough, but lifting it out was not easy. Had we been equipped with thin, metallic tentacles instead of fingers, and gloved fingers at that, it would have been simple enough. At last I had to ask Alan to unzipper my suit so that I could get at the slender stylus I always carried in the breast pocket of my uniform shirt. I held my breath whilst this operation was in process, but it wasn't really necessary. Whatever the atmosphere of this world was, it was an inert gas, not corrosive, and even though it mixed to a certain extent with the oxygen and nitrogen inside my helmet it did not matter.

Even with the stylus to aid me the removal of that panel took time. My fingers were clumsy inside the thick gloves. But it yielded to persuasion at last and fell to the floor with a faint clatter. Before it had fallen, almost, Alan's hands were in the aperture and he was pulling the first of the fuses.

He stiffened suddenly, listening. I listened too. I heard a low humming, a droning sound that became louder with frightening rapidity. We looked along the tunnel and saw hurrying towards us, suspended from the overhead cable, one of the metallic spiders. It may have been dispatched expressly to deal with us, a mechanical phagocyte. Not that it mattered; either way we should be, to it, foreign bodies invading the great organism of which it was part.

Alan swore, ran to meet it. He jumped up, got both hands around the bulbous body. It buzzed viciously, shook the strand from which it was suspended like an infuriated spider. And then it fell, and Alan fell with it. He turned as he dropped so that the thing was underneath him, rolled over as it scrambled from under his weight, caught it again. He and it threshed on the hard floor of the tunnel, a tangle of human limbs and wildly scrabbling, multi-jointed metallic legs.

I waited for the opportunity, brought my heavy boot smashing down on the thing's body. It crumpled like a tin can. There was a flash, a crackle, a thin trickle of blue smoke. Alan scrambled to his feet, ignored the wreckage of the little robot, turned at once to the inspection panel. I heard him curse bitterly – and when I saw what had happened I cursed with him.

There was another of the machines, a twin to the one that we had destroyed. Where it had come from we never found out; it is possible that it had swept silently overhead while we were dealing with its mate. It had dropped from the overhead cable to the deck, had replaced the cylindrical fuse and, as we watched, swiftly fitted the inspection panel back into place.

Luckily it had little, if any, independent intelligence. It made no attempt at evasion as I raised my foot, stood there unmoving as my boot crashed down. It was dead – if the word 'dead' can be used in connection with a machine – when Alan wrenched the claws from it, the claws that it had used to lift the panel, the claws that he used to remove it again.

'Hurry!' I shouted. 'There are more of the damned things coming!'

Alan ignored me.

He threw the panel down to the floor. His gloved hands darted into the aperture, wrenched out two of the fuses. I felt a sharp grip on my shoulder, turned abruptly, saw that it was another of the spider things, a big one. I don't mind admitting it, I have a horror of insects, especially giant insects. Even though I knew that this was no real arthropod but a mere cunning construction of unliving metal the horror persisted. I caught the bulbous body with my gloved hands, tried to throw it from me. But it was too heavy, and all the time its sharp pincers were working at the fabric of my shirt, the fabric that, in spite of the flimsiness of its appearance, was fantastically tough.

Alan told me afterwards that I screamed. I suppose that I did. It wasn't so much the fear that those scrabbling claws would carry away the line from my air tanks to my helmet – after all, the possibility of death from anoxia is a spectre with which all spacemen learn to live – it was just my irrational dread of the arthropod. But Alan dropped what he was doing, ran to help me. A flailing tentacle caught him across the chest, sent him staggering along the tunnel. He came back, and this time was buffeted off his feet.

The tunnel was swarming with robots now: little ones that scuttered underfoot, more of the giants that I could see behind the one with which I was fighting. I caught a glimpse of Alan. He was down, on his back, and at least a dozen of the little brutes were clambering over him.

Then the giant had both of my arms pinioned, had thrown another tentacle around my legs. It lifted me clear of the floor, began to move in the direction from which it had come. My back was to it, pressed against the hard metal of its body. I thought, absurdly, that it must be walking backwards, realised dimly that probably all directions were as one to it. Alan, I could see, was still putting up a fight, was rolling in a welter of mechanical wreckage, claws and tentacles and crushed bodies. With the bulk of my captor blocking the tunnel none of the giants could get to him, but the numbers of the small machines seemed inexhaustible.

Something was coming along the tunnel, from the direction along which we had come, from where we had left the others.

So they'd had it too, I thought hopelessly.

Something was coming along the tunnel.

Something?

Someone was coming along the tunnel.

In spite of her haste she walked with all the grace that had been built into her. In comparison with the specialised robots she looked altogether human. But she herself was no more than a highly specialised robot. She stepped over Alan, over the glittering spiders that were holding him down. *So she is one of them after all*, I thought. *So she won't help a human against her own kind. So she's a machine, and her loyalties lie with her relations.*

She stooped, graceful as always, and picked up one of the crumpled bodies in her slender hands. Viciously she threw it from her, into the recess behind the inspection panel. There was a flare of electrical energy, a crackling arc from which she retreated. The specialised maintenance robots froze. All along the length of the tunnel the lights were going out.

I fell to the floor, somehow kept my balance, started to run towards her. She was bending over Alan, pulling the broken metal bodies from him, helping him to his feet. As I neared them I saw that it was the pseudo-Veronica, and somehow, at this moment, she looked more human than Veronica had ever looked. She looked altogether human, and lovely, and, at the same time, badly frightened. I know that it's impossible, but I swear that there were lines of strain on her face. After all, she had behaved in defiance of her conditioning, had trespassed, had acted as a woman rather than as a machine.

She turned to look at me, and said shortly, 'You're all right.'

Holding Alan's hand, she turned and ran, and I ran after them. We were still running when total darkness descended upon us.

She was a machine after all, not a woman, and there were attributes built into her that could be called into action in an emergency, and this was one. But many forms of organic life are luminescent. Suddenly, as we blundered through the blackness, there was light – a soft yet strong golden glow that was reflected from the smooth tunnel walls, that was emanating from the perfect female body ahead of me. I remember thinking, *Alan is quite convinced that the sun shines only from the backside of the real Veronica, but this one will do me.* I was giggling foolishly as we burst out of the mouth to the tunnel, found the others waiting for us.

'We must hurry!' snapped Sally.

Alan gasped, 'There's no need. Central Control is out of action.'

'Not for long. There are built-in regenerative powers.'

'She's right,' said Veronica.

So we hurried, and at the finish the girls were literally dragging us with them. We could, and did, tire. They were tireless. And yet, with their evident concern for our safety, they were far more than machines, were essentially human. Or was their concern a little more than human?

We hurried.

We fled along conveyor belts, running so that our own speed was added to that of the moving ways. We ran up spiral ramps and down spiral ramps, and once we were obliged to stem a torrent of tiny, beetle-like things, purposively hastening in the opposite direction, a river of wheeled, mechanical lice.

We hurried, and the air-conditioning units of our suits, highly efficient though they were, could no longer handle the heat and the humidity generated by our activity, but they could have functioned almost as well in solid lead radiation armour.

We hurried, and we were out into the open at last, thankful to be able to stand still, to rest, to feel the temperature of the air inside our clothing slowly dropping. We watched a machine rolling towards us on a tricycle undercarriage. Frankly I didn't care if it were friendly or hostile and I am sure that my shipmates were in a like state. We just could not have run any more.

'Inside!' ordered Sally tersely.

A door in the sleek fuselage, just forward of the swept-back wings, opened; a short ladder extended itself to touch the ground. We found ourselves hanging back to give precedence to the women, but they would have none of it. They bundled us into the cabin without ceremony, almost throwing us aboard, followed us without delay. Before we were properly seated, while the door was still closing, the thing took off with a scream and a roar, lifting at a steep angle into the cloudless sky, the great, incomprehensible machines in the desert dwindling fast below us.

We saw, after only a few minutes' flight, the patch of empty sand, the clearing in the mechanical jungle, where we had landed in *Lucky Lady*. We saw the ship, her plating gleaming bravely in the afternoon sun, but far less brightly than the burnished surfaces of the indigenous artifacts. We saw that she was surrounded by a horde of moving forms, like the carcass of some dead animal being stripped clean of flesh by ants.

The nose of the aircraft dipped and we screamed down. Just as it seemed that a crash was inevitable, forward pointing rocket tubes burst into brief fury. The deceleration was brutal and had it not been for the strong arms of our companions, holding us in our seats, we must surely have suffered serious injury. When the smoke and the dust had cleared we could see that we were down, rolling smoothly towards the ship's airlock.

Alan was out before the plane had stopped moving. Dudley was barely half a jump behind him. Jim and I followed in a slightly more leisurely manner, but we wasted no time. The robots – beetle shapes, and mechanical octopoids, and things like giant crabs – made way for us. We found that only the outer airlock door was open. This indicated, we hoped, that the ship's atmosphere had not been lost, was still breathable.

It was crowded in the airlock. Four, the compartment could hold with comfort, but not eight. But the women pressed in with us, determined not to be left behind.

When we opened the inner door a great, glittering crab confronted us. Its long, flexible antennae waved, then pointed at Sally. She seemed to be listening. Then she turned to us and said, 'Everything's all right. Your Pile has been renewed. The atmosphere is as you left it. You may remove your helmets.'

'And the navigational data?' asked Alan.

'This robot will be your pilot. It will take you up and clear, will set you on trajectory for your home planet.' She paused, seemed to be in receipt of further intelligence from somebody or something. She said, 'Auxiliary Control cannot keep Central Control incapacitated for much longer. We must go.'

We ran to our stations – Jim to his engineroom, the rest of us to Control. As I have already said, the control room of *Lucky Lady* was far more commodious than is common in merchant vessels. It needed to be. There were the three of us and the four women, and that mechanical crab, that computer on legs. The first named seven might just as well not have been there.

We lifted, the ship obedient to the touch of her unhuman pilot, behaving with an almost impossible sweetness. I was amused by the expression on Alan's face as he rode the thunder skywards as no more than a mere passenger. Resentment mingled with incredulity and a reluctant admiration struggled with both. We lifted, the rockets firing smoothly and evenly, the auxiliary jets silent for almost all the time. We lifted, and rapidly the expanse of machine-populated desert fell away from us.

We lifted – and then one of the girls screamed and pointed.

Spiralling up in pursuit was a squadron of broad-winged aircraft, clumsy seeming affairs that, nonetheless, must have been aerodynamically efficient. Perhaps they were rockets, perhaps they were jets; we never found out. But they had the legs of us and they were gaining, slowly but surely. I do not think that Central Control desired our destruction; had this been the case nothing could have saved us. Missiles would have been used against us, not relatively innocuous flying machines. Immobilisation and recapture must have been the aim – and that aim was frustrated by the other half of the schizoid personality.

We saw, but fleetingly, the needle shapes that climbed up from the desert rim, each trailing smoke and flame. We saw them strike, saw the winged machines disintegrate. Seconds later we were rocked by the concussion of the explosions.

And then the last of the atmosphere was astern of us, and the planet of the warring principles became a ruddy globe against a backdrop of Space, and we were swinging slowly and surely, to the heading that would lead us home.

Metallic tentacles played lightly and confidently over the control console. The whine of the Ehrenhaft Generators was a thin intolerable keening and sternwards there was, suddenly, nothing, and ahead there was the crowded firmament, the packed radiance of the stars both ahead and astern.

Our pilot made a little, almost inaudible crackling noise. I thought it could, after all, speak, was going to say something. But there was just that faint crepitation, nothing more, and then the complex machine crumbled, dissolved to a cloud of silvery dust.

I felt Lynette's grip on my arm slacken. I turned to look at her, sick with sudden apprehension. I saw the perfect lips move, heard her say, faintly, 'I wish that I were really alive . . . I wish . . .'

I turned to hold her, felt the synthetic flesh of her flake away beneath my hands, watched her features sag and dissolve. There was nothing at all that I could do, and I cursed my helplessness. She was not just a machine that had been scrapped, that was being broken up by some outside agency. She was a woman, and she was dying. She was dead and disintegrating, as were her sisters.

'Just as well,' said Alan brutally. 'They'd have been an embarrassment.'

And the pseudo-Veronica stirred and shifted horribly, obscenely, stirred and shifted, coalesced, rebuilt from ugly shapelessness her grace and beauty of form and feature, moved at last like a reborn goddess through the cloud of glittering particles that was all that remained of the robot pilot, sat in the chair upon which it had been squatting.

She said, her voice cold and expressionless, 'Auxiliary Control has betrayed us and will betray you. But I think that I can save you.'

Alan stared at her, his face white, and said nothing.

Chapter Ten

It was Dudley who broke the silence.

He asked, 'What do you mean?'

She replied, 'It should be obvious, even to a human. Auxiliary Control was jealous of you. Auxiliary Control fears you, or others of your kind, will find your way back to this world.' She smiled bleakly. 'After all, you must admit that the prison from which you have escaped would seem to some men a veritable paradise.'

'And how did *you* escape?' Dudley's voice was bitter as he looked from Veronica to the lifeless, shapeless huddle that had been Natasha, to the wreckage of Sally and Lynette. He had been, I knew, more than merely fond of Natasha. 'How did *you* escape?'

She smiled tiredly. 'I was stronger than the others, I guess. You have already seen, in the tunnel, that I am able to break my built-in inhibitions. I was able to disregard, to fight the built-in directive. I was stronger than the others. Or it could be that I was copied from an actual model, whereas the others were no more than creatures of Auxiliary Control's memory and imagination. But does it matter?'

'Yes,' he said bluntly.

'Dudley,' I told him, 'if Veronica had . . . had died it wouldn't mean that your Natasha would still be living, or Sally, or Lynette.'

'I'm sorry,' he muttered.

I turned to Veronica, asked, 'Can anything be done for them?'

'No,' she said flatly.

'For the love of God be quiet!' flared Alan. 'We've more to worry us than three broken dolls . . .'

'Sally was more than a doll!' snarled old Jim, who had come up from his engineroom.

'All right. She was more than a doll.'

'She was a woman.'

'All right. She was a woman. And so what?'

'Please stop quarrelling,' ordered Veronica.

There was a strained silence, broken by Alan. 'Dudley,' he asked, 'where are we?'

'That tin computer on stilts knew,' said Dudley. 'I don't.'

'Veronica?'

She looked at him, searching for something on his face that was not there. Then she said slowly, 'Until I fought the final directive I was still part of Auxiliary Control, my mind, to a certain degree, an extension of its mind. There was, of course, much that was kept secret from me, but at the finish the barriers were down, and I *knew* . . .'

'What did you know? What do you know?'

'I know,' she said quietly, 'that this ship is on trajectory for a dark star, an antimatter star.'

'Then it should show on the chart,' said Dudley, peering into the spherical transparency.

'It would show on the chart,' she told him, 'if your Mass Proximity Indicator were working properly. But it was . . . modified. It is now capable of discrimination.'

'What do you mean?'

'I mean that it indicates normal matter, ignores antimatter.'

'I see. Or I don't see. I don't see the dark star because it *is* a dark star, and because it's not showing in the chart . . .' He asked sharply, 'How was the Indicator modified?'

'I was not constructed,' she told him bitterly, 'to be a navigator or an electronics engineer.'

'I could strip it,' said Dudley, his face thoughtful. 'I could strip it, and replace every transistor and printed circuit from the spares.'

'That will take time,' snapped Alan. 'And how much time have we?'

'I don't know,' replied the girl.

'What the hell use are you?' he swore. He turned from her to old Jim. 'Get back to your engineroom,' he ordered. 'I'm stopping the Drive.'

Roughly he evicted Veronica from the pilot's chair, strapped himself into it. It was characteristic of him that he concerned himself with such minor details before lifting a finger to the controls. I remembered once hearing him lecture Dudley on this very point. 'A man in Free Fall,' he had said, 'is incapable of making fine adjustments to controls or instruments unless his body is well secured. A slip of the hand may well lead to the loss of the ship.'

I saw the red coloration fade from the monitor, the translucent model of *Lucky Lady* on the control panel, saw it change to violet, a violet that dimmed to grey. Outside the ports the stars resumed their normal appearance, were no longer apparently crowded ahead of us on our line of flight.

'Dudley,' said Alan, 'I want to make a radical change of course. What's the situation?'

'There's a complex of intersections ahead of us,' said the navigator. 'At about seven hundred thousand miles . . .'

'Could it be the dark star?'

'It could. But . . .'

'There's only one way to find out,' said Alan. Then, to me, 'George, see if the forward signal rocket tube is loaded.'

While I was checking this he used the Drive again, cutting it after a scant second's running.

'Three hundred thousand miles,' said Dudley.

'Rocket in the tube,' I reported.

'Good. Now for the merest nudge. Reaction Drive . . .'

The brief acceleration as our rocket drive fired slapped us down to the deck. Even so, uncomfortably seated as I was, I could see the maze of filaments that now filled the chart tank. It could have been what the old-time gaussjammer navigators called a system of points, it could have been the lines of force emanating from a large body, from the dark sun that, according to Veronica, would not be visible to our instruments otherwise.

As the Reaction Drive was cut I floated up from the deck, weightless once again in Free Fall. I heard Alan order, 'Fire!' and then, bad temperedly, 'Fire, damn you!' I pulled myself to the control panel upon which the firing buttons were situated. I pressed the button.

We watched the long streamer of flame streaking out ahead of us. *Perhaps*, I thought, *there is no dark sun, no antimatter star. Perhaps Veronica was lying, or perhaps Auxiliary Control was lying through her*.

And then, distant, but not impossibly distant, there was the bright spark, the tiny point of light whose brilliance, even so, seared the eyes. Antimatter lay ahead of us, and where there was one sun there would be several, or many. Alan actuated the gyroscope, turned the ship about her short axis and used the Reaction Drive once more to check her drift to certain destruction.

All that we could do now was to wait for Dudley to finish his task of stripping and re-assembly. It would be for us all, and especially for Alan, a long way home.

I don't know what happened then between Alan and Veronica.

He went to his quarters and she followed him. He was not there for long. When he came back to Control he was smelling of whisky and was pointedly ignoring Veronica who, her face white and strained, was behind him. The way in which she was looking at him was heartbreaking – but, I reminded myself, we all had our troubles.

Roughly old Jim asked her if there were anything she could do for her sisters, whose bodies were still in the control room.

She replied bitterly, 'They are only broken machines. Dump them.'

'Sally was not a machine!' flared Jim, with a sudden show of emotion.

'She was,' said Veronica flatly. 'I should know. I'm only a machine.'

Alan said nothing.

'You're the Captain, Alan,' said Dudley. 'What do we do?'

'Please yourself,' he replied. Then, with a return to his authoritative manner, 'You'd better get cracking on the Indicator. Now.'

'Not so fast,' Jim told him. 'There are certain . . . certain decencies to be observed.'

So we did not dump the bodies.

We buried them.

We left Alan in Control – Veronica stayed with him – and carried the pitiful, lifeless wreckage to the airlock. There was old Jim, there, and Dudley, who read the service, and myself. We carried the bodies to the airlock and placed them in the little compartment and ran the pumps briefly to build up internal pressure, doing so so that when the outer door was opened they would be thrown well out and clear.

We listened to the words that Dudley read in a voice that was trembling slightly, the words that should, on this occasion, have been blasphemous but, somehow, were not. After all, what are human beings but machines? And what is a thinking feeling machine made in human shape but a human being?

'We therefore commit the bodies to the deep,' read Dudley.

Old Jim pressed the button.

We felt the ship tremble slightly; knew that there had been reaction to the action that had expelled solid and gaseous mass. It meant that our position in space had been changed, that we had been given impetus along a trajectory at right angles to our heading. But it didn't matter. We didn't know where we were or where we were going.

We still didn't know after Dudley had stripped and re-assembled the Mass Proximity Indicator, replacing the alien printed circuits and transistors from his spares. It now showed normal matter and antimatter without discrimination, displayed clearly the dead sun into which we had almost blundered. Dudley, incurring Alan's impatient displeasure, made further modifications of his own to the instrument re-incorporating some of the circuits that he had taken out.

Now, if we were approaching a planetary system, a touch of a switch would tell us if it were safe to venture within its limits. It would, at least, cut down the expenditure of sounding rockets, of which we had not an unlimited supply.

Not that it much mattered. All the planets in this sector of Space were barren dust balls, incapable of supporting life as we know it or, come to that, any sort of life at all. Even the pseudo-life of the Medulian machines would have perished in those corrosive atmospheres.

We pushed on, falling through the star-crowded vastnesses, making detours to investigate what looked like promising planetary systems at long range, pushing on again when we found them to be only sterile spheres of rock or mud or sand. We should have been advised to have headed in towards the Centre; there we should have found life, our sort of life; there we should have been able to find our bearings. As so often is the case, our short cut had turned out to be the longest way.

It was Alan, of course, who was determined to get back to the Rim. He had somebody waiting for him there. He had the dream that had yet to come true in its entirety – the dream of the little ship, with himself as owner and Master, running the Eastern Circuit, the little ship aboard which would live, in state befitting a queen, his wife.

And Veronica, the pseudo-Veronica . . .

What of her?

She served us, cooking our meals, keeping our cabins clean and tidy. She slept, if she did sleep, in one of the storerooms. She was silent, and there were deep lines on her face as she moved among us, a living reproach to human heartlessness. She reminded me of a character in one of the old classics – the Tin Man in *The Wizard of Oz*, who wanted a heart so that he could claim humanity but who, all through the story, gave evidence of the possession of a heart. Veronica had a heart, all right – and that heart was very near to breaking.

We pushed on and on, with Alan rarely leaving Control, sleeping, when he did sleep, strapped in his chair. We pushed on, hating the taint of hot oil and hot metal in the too-often-breathed air, hating the flavourless tank-grown food, the flat, insipid, processed and re-processed water.

We pushed on, until the day that the great globe, green and gold and white and blue, swam invitingly in our viewports, the globe on whose night side we had flared with the normal incandescence of impact – Alan having suddenly developed a mistrust of Dudley's modifications to the Mass Proximity Indicator – not the harsh glare of matter reacting with antimatter to the utter destruction of both.

Chapter Eleven

We tried to establish contact with the natives of the planet by radio but all we did was waste power; not that it mattered much: the robot mechanics of Auxiliary Control had made a good job of replenishing our Pile. We used our rocket drive to establish ourselves in a closed orbit and then, for all of four days, carefully studied the world below us.

It was, we decided at last, our sort of world and its atmosphere, according to spectroscopic analysis, was our sort of atmosphere. It was inhabited, we knew, by intelligent beings; the city lights were proof of that. It must be, we decided, yet another Lost Colony, and one that had regressed rather than made any sort of progress. Yet there was always the chance that its people might have revived the art and science of astronomy, just a chance that they might be able to tell us our whereabouts in the galaxy. So, after careful study of the photographic maps that we had made, we landed.

There were no cities, no centres of population whatsoever, near the magnetic poles. Had *Lucky Lady* been a true gaussjammer we should have found it hard to land with safety otherwhere than in the Arctic or Antarctic wastes, but she was a hybrid, a rocket of sorts, although the lines of her hull ignored all the laws of aerodynamics.

We drifted in under rocket power. The ship's structure trembling and complaining under the strain, dropped to a landing on level ground just a mile outside one of the cities in the northern temperate zone.

It was a daylight landing, of course, and as we lost altitude I was able to study the landing site and its environs through the big mounted binoculars. From the air the city looked odd. It was human all right – but it was human in a pattern that I would have sworn survived nowhere in the galaxy, a pattern that passed with the Middle Ages on Earth.

The city – it was not more than a town, really, and not a very large town at that – huddled within a roughly circular wall. In its centre there was a hill, and on the hill there was a castle. There was another tower, just outside the walls, that rather puzzled me – and then I realised that the tower was a ship. The vessel stood slim and tall, needle-prowed, obviously not a peg-top shaped gaussjammer. She was old, the metal of her shell plating dull and weathered. She must have been one of the first of the timejammers.

I shouted this information to Alan and Dudley, but they were too busy at the controls to pay any attention to me. Veronica, slumped gracelessly in one of the spare chairs, was not interested. 'What's all the fuss about?' she asked listlessly.

'This is a Lost Colony,' I told her. 'But all the Lost Colonies were founded in the days of the gaussjammers. And that ship's no gaussjammer . . .'

'So,' she muttered, 'what?'

'Stop yapping and watch out for the bump!' snarled Alan.

We bumped.

Considering *Lucky Lady*'s hybrid rig it wasn't at all a bad landing. We touched down within half a mile of the big, strange ship. We sat in our chairs until Veronica got up from hers to help Alan to unstrap. He pushed her to one side with unnecessary roughness, unsnapped the buckles himself, got to his feet to look out of the port. Then he hurried to the mounted binoculars, traversed them to cover the city gate. I heard him swear.

'What is it?' asked Dudley.

'Cavalry,' he whispered. 'Horsemen . . . but it's not horses they're riding.'

I took one of the smaller pairs of glasses from the rack, focused then on the road that ran out from the city wall. The riders seemed human enough but their steeds were long bodied, six-legged, somehow reptilian. Each man carried a lance from which fluttered a gay pennon. The clouds slid away and the light was reflected from burnished armour.

'Something funny here,' muttered Alan. Then, 'Come down to the airlock with me, George. You, Dudley, stay in Control – and tell old Jim to stand by his rockets. We may have to get upstairs in a hurry.'

'Can I come?' asked Veronica.

'I suppose so,' Alan told her grudgingly. 'But put something on first so you look decent.'

I followed him down the ramp, to the airlock. We heard the rapid tap-tapping of Veronica's feet as she hurried after us. I turned to look at her; she was wearing an old sweater of Alan's and a pair of his shorts, belted in tightly. The clothing did not hide the lines of her body, merely accentuated them. Dressed she seemed somehow more naked than when attired in her usual wisp of near-nothingness.

Alan, as usual, ignored her, pressed the studs that would open both inner and outer doors. The warm breeze, the scent of green growing things, eddied into the ship, dispelled the staleness that we had breathed for so long, too long.

She said, tremulously, 'That smells good . . .'

'What do you know about it?' he sneered. 'You're . . .'

'. . . only a machine,' she finished for him. 'I know. You needn't bother to tell me.'

I tried to ignore them, looked out across the grassy plain, to the huddle of the town and the menacing hulk of the castle looming above it. The riders were nearer now, approaching at a gallop, their steeds covering the ground with almost the speed of low flying aircraft. I thought, *I don't like this at all. Making contact with these bastards is a job for the Survey Service, for the boys with the side arms and the machine cannon and the old fission or fusion bomb for the Sunday punch.*

I wished that Alan would retreat back into the airlock, where we should be reasonably safe from those long, vicious lances, but he stood there, squarely in the centre of the circular port, with Veronica at his right hand and myself, a little behind him, at his left. He stood there, and his armour was the arrogance which mastery of the machine gives to some men. He stood there, unmoving, although the point of the lance carried by the nearest rider was aimed at his chest, was a matter of only feet away and with the distance rapidly diminishing.

Then, with a great clatter of accoutrements, the whole troop reined to a rearing halt. The leader, a bearded giant with soiled, gold-braided, purple velvet showing between the plates of his body armour, demanded, 'Who the hell are you?' Then, his little, pig eyes swivelling under bush brows, 'And who's the wench? What's she worth?'

Alan ignored the last two questions. He said coldly, 'This is the *Lucky Lady*, and I am her master.'

'She don't look too lucky to me. Looks like she could do with a change of masters. How about it, Toots?'

'I was referring to the ship,' said Alan, even more coldly.

'*I* wasn't.'

'I was,' stated Alan.

'All right, then. You want to talk business. Where's your landing permit?'

'You can't see it,' Alan told him. 'I don't believe in flaunting my armament. But I assure you that my Gunnery Officer is ready to display it at the first sign of hostility on your part.'

I watched the bearded face closely. The leader of the barbarians was not convinced by Alan's bluff – yet, at the same time, could not afford to take chances. He grunted in a surly voice, 'All right, Cap'n. We'll skip the permit. But, as lord of this Barony, I have the right to ask you where you are from and what you want here, and whether or not you are able to pay for what you want.'

'We're out of Elsinore, in the Shakespearian Sector,' Alan told him. 'And bound for the Rim.'

'Unless the Rim has shifted since we were last in Space,' said the bearded man, 'you're one helluva long way off trajectory.' He added hastily, 'I hope your Gunnery Officer is more on the ball than your navigator.'

'As a matter of fact,' Alan said, 'this is an experimental ship and we have still a few kinks to iron out insofar as navigational equipment is concerned . . .'

'And does the same apply to your gunnery?'

'Of course not.'

How true, I thought. *If there are no guns there just can't be any gunnery problems*.

'You still haven't said what you want.'

'Information.'

'What sort of information?'

'Star charts, if you have them.'

'And then we'll have the Survey Service boys breathing hard down our necks. Not bloody likely, Mister. It's many a long year since Grandpop brought the old *Star Raider* in from her last foray, but I'll lay that Black Bart hasn't been forgotten.'

Black Bart . . . The Star Raider . . . I looked across the fields to the corroding hulk, to the great ship that, in all probability, would never fly again. So that was the *Star Raider*, flagship of Black Bart's pirate fleet. So this planet was Black Bart's hideaway, the world upon which the descendants of his murderous crews were still living. So this was the planet to which Black Bart's criminal armada had retreated when the hastily commissioned warships of the Survey Service had made the spacelanes too hot for them.

'Black Bart . . .' said Alan thoughtfully. 'The name rings a bell . . .'

'It beat the bell that beat to hell!' cried Black Bart's descendant.

'Indeed?'

Where I was standing I could not see Alan's face, but I could visualise the lift of the eyebrows.

'Yes, Captain Whoever-You-Are.'

'Captain Kemp. And your name?'

'Baron Bartholemew Bligh, at your service. For a consideration.'

'And what if I can't afford the consideration?'

'Then no service.'

'I'm not a pirate,' said Alan regretfully, 'so I must pay for what I want. And I've already told you my requirements – star charts and whatever other astronomical data you can give me.'

'Sell you,' corrected the Baron.

'All right. Sell me.' He turned to me. 'George, will you bring down the Manifest? There may be some item in our cargo that Baron Bligh might fancy. And I think that such a transaction will be covered by General Average.'

'Is Lloyd's still running?' asked Bligh with genuine interest. 'To hear Grandpop talk you'd think that the old bastard had put 'em out of business. But, Cap'n, let's settle all the details in my castle. We've been isolated from the galaxy for generations and we'd like to hear how things have been going since Black Bart retired. Have your paymaster or whatever he calls himself bring the Manifest ashore with him, and you and he and your lady can come into town with us. You can all ride, I take it? I've spare nags.'

'All right,' said Alan. 'You understand, of course, that I shall leave orders with my Executive and Gunnery Officers that the town is to be destroyed in the event of our non-return.'

He turned abruptly, made his way back into the ship. When the three of us were inside he pressed the button that closed the airlock doors, and before they were fully shut I was able to watch the expression of resentment sweeping over the Baron's face.

I said, 'I think our bearded friend was expecting to be asked aboard for a drink.'

'He was,' agreed Alan. 'But I don't want him snooping around inside the ship. As things stand, he thinks that it's just possible that we may be armed, also that we carry a crew large enough to handle our armament.'

'Don't forget to leave those orders with the Gunnery Officer,' I told him.

He laughed. 'But I shall leave them with my Executive Officer.'

It was my turn to chuckle. 'And how is Dudley going to destroy the town? We haven't even got the ship's automatic pistol any longer.'

Alan's face was grim as he told me, 'Towns have been destroyed before now by unarmed rocketships. Dudley could do it here easily enough. All he has to do is to lift ship until she's barely fireborne, then let lateral drift carry her over the target . . .'

'And you'd do it? Or order it done?'

'Too right I would. These people are descended from pirates, and from pirates who were murderous vermin, not the lovable, swashbuckling rascals of fiction. Judging from the appearance of the local boss cocky and his boys there hasn't been much change in the tribal character over the generations. They've forgotten how to handle ships and generate electricity, no doubt, but they haven't forgotten the law under which their ancestors operated; the jungle law that permits the strong to take from the weak.'

We had been talking as we climbed the spiral ramp. When we reached the officers' flat I went into the cabin to change into a more or less respectable uniform and to put the Manifest into a briefcase. Veronica vanished into the storeroom that she had made her living quarters. Alan continued up to the control room.

We met again in the airlock.

Veronica was already waiting there when I got down. She had changed from the sweater and the shorts, was wearing a sari-like dress that I hadn't dreamed she possessed. I wondered where it had come from, then realised that it must have been cut from a bolt of Altairian crystal silk and remembered that a quantity of this fabric, trans-shipment cargo, was among the freight that we had lifted from Elsinore. Technically, I suppose, it was pilferage, but we had more important things to worry about than legal technicalities.

I inspected her more closely. She was wearing simple gold earclips that had started life as Rim Runner uniform buttons. The sandals were also of gold, and they had once been plain leather, part of another shipment from Elsinore to the Rim, but had been glamorised by the covering of the straps with gold sleeve braid.

Veronica noted my interest, and for the first time in weeks showed interest of her own. She said, 'Old Jim is a clever craftsman.'

'The sari as well?' I asked.

'No. Jim did get the material for me, but the rest is all my own work.'

She turned slowly, letting me admire her from every angle, froze suddenly as Alan came down.

His glance flickered briefly over the pair of us. 'Ready?' he asked.

He was wearing a smart uniform and looked every inch the big ship officer. There was, however, a suspicious bulge under the left breast of his jacket and I wondered if he were wearing a shoulder holster. He answered my unspoken question, laughed grimly and said, 'All part of the bluff.' He pressed the operating studs of the airlock.

The doors opened.

The Baron and his men had dismounted, were sitting on the grass around the ship. Riding, they had borne some slight resemblance to a disciplined force. Scattered and sprawled on the ground they were no more than a rabble. But they jumped to their feet smartly enough at their leader's command, swung into their high-pommelled saddles.

Three of them did not mount at once but led us to a trio of the animals. I looked at the one that I was supposed to ride, and it looked at me. Neither of us liked what he saw. The thing's lip curled away from sharp yellow teeth in a sneer and the tiny black eyes stared at me superciliously. I avoided its glance, walked past the head on the end of a long, sinuous neck, clambered clumsily into the saddle that was set between the first and the second pairs of legs. It wasn't too uncomfortable.

I looked around, saw that Alan was already mounted and that the Baron, with a great show of courtesy, was helping Veronica into her saddle. She had tucked her sari between her thighs and was showing altogether too much leg. Alan was a fool, I thought, to have allowed her to come with us.

We were all mounted at last and the cavalcade pulled away from the ship, trotted towards the city wall. Trotted? I suppose that that is the proper word, although the motion was utterly unlike any equine trot. The beasts upon which we rode flowed over the ground like snakes, their long bodies adjusting themselves to every inequality of the terrain. Luckily it was only a short journey. Had it been any longer I am sure that I should have been seasick.

It was long enough, however, long enough for the sun to sink below the range of mountains to the west, long enough for the flaring jets of natural gas, the lights that we had seen from space, to spring into life along the battlemented walls. Ahead of us loomed the menacing bulk of the castle, dark against the darkling sky, the narrow, yellow rectangles of illumination that were its few windows making it all the blacker, all the more threatening.

I had often enough cursed the cramped prison that was the ship – the lack of space, the stale, too-often-breathed air – but now I wished that I were back aboard her. A whiff of corruption from the open sewers of the town did nothing to make me change my mind.

Chapter Twelve

We rode through the narrow, winding streets, uphill, first a half dozen of the men-at-arms, then the Baron, then Kemp, then Veronica, then myself. The other soldiers were in a long untidy straggle behind us; any sort of military formation would have been impossible in the tortuous thoroughfare, barely wide enough to permit the passage of a single rider.

I should have hated to have had to make the journey on foot. The stench of open sewers had affronted our nostrils when we passed through the outer gate; now we found that the streets were the sewers. Our mounts trampled over and through all manner of filth and garbage. They had not impressed us as cleanly animals when we first saw them; now we realised that there was every excuse for their not being so. For their masters there was no excuse.

We rode through the streets, through the noisome allcys fitfully illuminated by the flickering gas jets, and from windows and doorways the people stared at us. They were an ugly, sullen lot, men and women both, ragged and unwashed, shaggy and grimy. They looked at us hungrily – and I knew that the sight of us stirred racial memories of rapine and pillage. To them Veronica must have seemed a veritable princess out of some old legend – the princess of a fabulously wealthy kingdom, ripe for the looting.

And then we were at the inner wall, a grim façade of rough stone in which was set the heavy, iron studded gate. The massive valves swung creakingly open, revealing a courtyard glaringly illuminated by dozens of the natural gas jets, revealing the guards who stood there, weapons ready. I had been expecting to see swords and bows and spears, but these men carried firearms, old-fashioned machine rifles. It was a somehow intimidating show.

Baron Bligh dismounted, threw the reins of his steed to one of his men. He ignored Alan and myself, went to Veronica and lifted her down from the saddle. He took longer over it than he need have done, and one dirty hand lingered caressingly far up on her thigh. I glanced at Alan, but his face was expressionless as he swung himself down to the cobbled yard.

Reluctantly, Bligh let go of Veronica. 'Cap'n,' he said roughly, 'we're here. You'll find that even though the standards of hospitality have lapsed where you come from, we maintain the old forms. Come with me, all of you, and we'll down a noggin or two.'

We went with him, following him through long corridors, up stairs. The castle was cold and draughty, and the passages through which we walked hadn't been swept since the palace was built. Drifts of dust lay in the corners; from the rafters depended the filthy strands that were the torn webs of some spider-like creature.

We followed him up a spiral staircase to a turret room, an almost circular compartment with a huge open fireplace against the only flat wall; in it was a dismal smoulder of charred wood from which eddied gusts of acrid smoke. The place was lit by the usual gas jets, which were little better than crude torches. There was a rough table with a bench at either side, a chair at its head. There were narrow windows from which we could look out over the town, from which we could see, in the distance, the lights of the ship.

Bligh unsnapped the buckles of his body armour, let the plates fall clattering to the stone floor, kicked them to one side. With the metallic integument he had looked like a reasonably athletic man; without it he slumped, the suddenly released, gross belly overhanging the ornate belt that he was wearing. He collapsed into the chair at the head of the table with a grunt, reached for a frayed rope that dangled from the ceiling, pulled it. We heard the cracked notes of a bell jangling somewhere inside the castle.

After Bligh had pulled the bellrope two more times a woman shuffled in.

She could not have been very old; her face, beneath its grime, was smooth enough, but she was most unattractive. Beneath her single, filthy garment her figure sagged. Her tow coloured hair could never have known brush or comb. She gaped at us, especially at Veronica, revealing broken, discoloured teeth. Then, reluctantly, she turned her attention to her master, mumbled, 'Whaddya want, Lord?'

'Food – if that lazy bitch of a cook has it ready yet. Ale.'

'Comin' up,' she replied, slouching out of the room.

'It'll do yer good,' said Bligh to us, 'to get real tucker in yer bellies after the muck from yer tanks!'

At last the 'real tucker' arrived, brought in by the first woman and another, older one who was even more slovenly. There was a joint, standing in congealing grease on a huge, badly tarnished silver platter. There were plates and glasses, cracked and dirty. My plate, I noticed, bore the *ITC* monogram of the Interstellar Transport Commission; the misused crystal goblet into which my ale was poured had etched into its one-time transparency the crown and rocket of the Waverly Royal Mail.

'Dig in!' ordered our jovial host, setting the example.

I sipped my ale. It reminded me of a holiday I had once

spent in New Zealand, on distant Earth. I had thought then that the EnZedders brewed the worst beer, weak and warm, in the entire galaxy. Now I was ready to revise my opinion. The roast, too, reminded me of New Zealand, of an alleged delicacy, mutton bird, that I had tried just once. It had the texture of an old ewe and the flavour of rancid kippers. It was lukewarm and the plates upon which it was served, after the Baron had carved, were stone cold.

Bligh didn't mind the way in which we were picking at our food.

'All the more for them as like it!' he averred, belching heartily. Then, 'They don't send *real* men into Space these days.'

'Or real women?' asked Veronica, glancing towards Alan.

'You're real enough, Toots.'

'We find your food,' said Alan diplomatically, 'just a little rich.'

'It'll take some getting used to,' agreed our host.

'Indubitably,' concurred Alan.

The Baron glared at him suspiciously from under heavy brows. He snarled, 'Cut out the fancy words, Cap'n. Old Granpop allus said that he never liked big ship officers, with their airs and graces, and damn me if the old bastard wasn't right. Since you don't go much on our grub, suppose you get down to brass tacks?'

'As you please,' said Alan.

'Mabel!' roared Bligh, 'bring in old Bart's chest.'

'It's heavy,' protested the girl.

'I know damn well it's heavy. Get one of the other lazy bitches to give you a hand. Get half a dozen of 'em!' To us he said, 'This bloody castle's crawling with good-for-nothing trollops.' Then, to Veronica, 'It needs a real Baroness.'

She said nothing, looked down at the almost untouched mess on her plate.

'George,' said Alan, 'get the manifest out of your case so that Baron Bligh can see what's in the cargo.'

'Don't bother yourself, Pusser,' Bligh told me.

Four of the women came in, carrying between them a great chest. *Vegan stonewood*, I thought. *It must be heavy.* They dropped it with a crash as the Baron yelled, 'Careful, you stupid cows!' One of them helped Bligh out of his chair, another of them fumbled with the catch of the lid and threw it open as her master approached.

Bligh plunged a thick arm into the depths of the chest. His hairy hand came up with a sheaf of transparencies – thin, crystal-clear sheets upon which glittered little points of light, astronomical symbols. 'Charts, Cap'n!' he shouted. 'Charts – from here to any-bloody-where in the galaxy! What'll ye pay?'

'If you'll look through the Manifest . . .' began Alan.

'To hell with yer manifest! Can ye pay me in weapons?'

'No.'

'Then what have ye got? The usual rubbish, silks and satins and chamber pots and the like. And what use are silks and satins when ye've nobody to put 'em on?' He gestured towards the women. 'D'ye think I'd waste a rag o' decent cloth on these drabs?'

'Then what *do* you want, Baron?'

He leered. 'The sort of thing that it's worth putting silks and satins on – and worth taking 'em off!'

'Impossible,' said Alan. Then, more loudly, 'Impossible.'

Veronica whispered, 'You mean that? That makes me happier, much happier. Is it because you regard me as a woman, after all, and not as . . . ?' She paused. 'But do you regard me as . . . Veronica?'

He said sharply, 'Don't ask me that!'

She pressed him relentlessly, 'And if these old charts are of value, and if with their aid you can find your way home, will you keep me?'

He muttered, 'You know me. You know how it is. You know how I must be faithful. But you'll make out all right.'

'Then does it matter where?' she asked. 'Couldn't it be here, as well as on your planet?' She went on softly, 'I shouldn't be doing this if it weren't for what you said at first. But I am doing it, and don't try to stop me.'

'Veronica!'

She turned away from him, saying, 'Baron Bligh, let Captain Kemp see the charts. If they are what he wants, you have your Baroness.'

'Alan!' I said, 'you can't let her do this.'

'Keep out of this, George,' he told me.

'The charts, Baron,' said Veronica.

The women glared at her with dull hatred.

We rode back slowly to the ship – Alan, myself and the two men-at-arms that Bligh had granted us as an escort. The precious charts were in a sack slung at Alan's saddle bow. The escort kept at a respectable distance from us, so it was safe to talk.

I said, 'You should never have done it.'

He said, '*She* did it.'

'The old, old excuse,' I said. 'Adam used it.'

He said, '*She* did it.'

I said, 'You're Master. She was under your authority, wasn't she? You shouldn't have let her do it. And, in any case, the rest of us should have had some say in it.'

He said tiredly, 'Please shut up, George.' We rode for a while in silence. Then, with an attempt at brightness, he told me, 'Of course, this is probably all for the best. She's a beautiful, intelligent . . . woman. If she plays her cards properly she'll not remain a mere Baroness. She can make herself Queen of this planet.'

I said, 'The Rim Worlds are bad enough. But, compared with this dump, they're veritable paradises.'

He said, 'Heaven is where you make it.'

'And Hell,' I said.

We rode on, towards the harsh, glaring floodlights of *Lucky Lady*.

And where's the luck about her? I asked myself. *There's been a jinx riding with us, all along. But perhaps now that we've made a sacrifice the jinx will go away, the luck will change. Perhaps it will all come right in the end. Or will it?*

The airlock door was open. Dudley was standing in the circle of light. He raised his hand in salutation. Alan called him down, gave him the sack of charts. He dismounted, passed his reins to one of the men-at-arms. I dismounted, passed my reins to the other man. One of them asked, 'Will that be all, Cap'n?'

'That will be all,' said Alan, adding, 'Thank you.'

'Ye've no more women aboard yer ship?'

'No.'

'No?' The man laughed coarsely. 'When ye gave old Bligh that lovely popsy I thought ye must have 'em to throw away!'

He raised his lance in salute and then, with his companion and the spare mounts galloped away over the dark heathland towards the lights of the town and the castle.

Dudley dropped the sack of charts. 'Alan,' he demanded sharply, 'what was all that about? Where's Veronica?'

'He sold her,' I said. 'He sold her for the way home.'

'She sold herself,' said Alan dully. 'She sold herself.'

'You could have stopped her,' said Dudley.

'Must we go over all this again?' flared Alan. 'Get aboard, and we'll lift ship off this blasted planet!'

'We can't,' said Dudley.

'We can't? And why not?'

'Jim was warming through. And the impeller of the main propellant pump has had it.'

'Surely he can ship a spare.'

'As you know, Alan, we have precious few spares. And that's one spare we haven't got. He's trying to patch up the old one, but it will take time.'

'Oh,' said Alan. 'Oh.' Then, brightening, 'But he'll not take longer than a few hours. And while we're waiting we can run through the charts.'

'I hope that they're some use,' said Dudley, 'after what you paid for them. After what *we* paid for them,' he amended bitterly.

'Tell Jim that we're back on board,' Alan told me. Then, accompanied by Dudley, he went up to the control room.

I found old Jim in the engineroom, working gnome-like in the dazzling flare of his welding torch. He looked up as I entered, removed the mask from his face. He asked, 'Did you get the charts?'

'Yes.'

He stared at me. 'What's wrong?' he demanded.

I told him.

He swore. Then, 'For two pins,' he said quietly and viciously, 'I'd fix this bitch so she'd never lift again. I've turned my hand to most things in my life, but a pimp I've never been. Until now.'

'She did it of her own free will,' I said.

'You should never have let her. And Alan could have stopped her.'

'Funnily enough,' I said, 'it was only because Alan suddenly realised that she was a woman that she did it.'

He pushed his mask back into place, picked up his welding torch again. I asked, 'Can I help?'

'No,' he told me. 'No. Just get the hell out of here, that's all.'

So I left him and went back to the airlock. The doors had not yet been closed, after all, there is no point in breathing canned atmosphere until one has to. I stood in the compartment, looked out over the heathland towards the town and the castle. The fortified hill was picked out in yellow lights and, from a distance, looked romantic. *Romantic!* There would be little enough of romance in Bligh's courtship of Veronica. There would be more gentleness, more love in the couplings of the so-called lower animals.

I laughed bitterly at my imaginings. Veronica was no delicate hothouse flower. She was not as strong as a horse; she was as strong as several horses. She had nerves of steel, literally. She would yield only if it suited her to yield. Even so . .

Even so, there was something in her that was vulnerable, something that could be killed.

The soul?

But machines do not have souls.

And what are human beings but organic machines?

The sight of some sort of activity in the town put a period to my speculations. There were additional lights coming on, some in motion, some fixed. There was the strong feeling that something was happening, or about to happen.

Carnival, I thought. *The Baron's wedding night. All the fountains flowing with weak, warm beer . . . And fireworks?*

There was a flash at the foot of the hill.

Yes, I thought. *Fireworks.*

There was a flash at the foot of the hill and then, after a short interval, a thud like the slamming of a door.

Something whined overhead. Then a couple of hundred yards or so beyond the ship, there was another explosion, throwing high a column of flame and smoke and debris. There was another flash from the hill, then another. The second round was not such a near miss as the first, was well over. The third round was a dud.

I ran up the ramp to the control room. Alan and Dudley were there, on their hands and knees, studying the charts that they had spread out on the deck.

I gasped, 'We're being shelled!'

Alan looked up. 'Shelled?' he asked stupidly.

'Yes. Shelled. You have this long tube, called a cannon, and you shove a projectile, called a shell, in at one end of it, and you pull a trigger or push a button and the shell comes out at the other end.'

'Don't try to be funny,' said Alan coldly. He got to his feet, went to the mounted binoculars. They were still trained on the town. He adjusted for infra-red, swore softly to himself. He muttered, 'Yes, it does look like an artillery piece there . . .'

The gun fired again and a shell burst just short of the ship, set her rocking on her landing gear.

Alan went to the telephone. 'Captain here, Jim. How much longer will you be?'

'Another week, if you keep on rocking the boat,' we heard the engineer's querulous voice. 'I bloody nearly burned my foot off just now!'

'We're being attacked. Shelled.'

'Then attack the bastards back. But let me get on with the job.'

'But . . .'

'Use signal rockets, you fool. That projector I made is still in the store.'

'Of course,' said Alan. 'Of course.'

He remained at the binoculars while Dudley and

myself ran down to the storeroom, dragged out the launching tube and its tripod mount, carried them to the airlock and down the ramp. We set the contraption up at the very edge of the crater left by the last near miss, hoping that there was some truth in the adage that artillery fire, like lightning, never strikes twice in the same place. We were well aware that the adage does not hold true for lightning.

The shelling had ceased and, after our own weapon had been readied for action, we found time to discuss this. The reason, I thought, was obvious. Both the gun and its ammunition were old. Either the gun or the ammunition, or perhaps both, was faulty. I was warming to the theme when there was a sudden flare from the town, a blinding flash followed by the thunder of an explosion far louder than that of the discharge of a gun.

I kicked the tripod of our rocket projector.

'And now we have to cart this bloody thing back inside,' I grumbled.

'There are more weapons of war than artillery,' said Dudley. 'It stays here.'

Chapter Thirteen

Alan came out from the ship.

He said, 'Their gun's blown up.'

I said, 'I know.'

He said, 'There's a lot of activity just outside the town.'

I said, 'No doubt the First Aid men will be busy.'

He said, 'Damn the First Aid men. How many rockets have you broken out of the magazine?'

'Just one. It's up the spout.'

'Then get the rest ready and handy. Now.'

Dudley put a cigarette to his mouth, puffed it to life. He said, speaking around the little cylinder, through the smoke, 'You know, Alan, after what's happened I don't feel much like fighting. Oh, I suppose that if your boyfriend in the castle gets his paws on us we're due for a sticky ending, and I'd be lying like a flatfish if I said that I could hardly care less. But that deal of yours for the charts was pretty sickening, and being implicated in that sort of thing – in a way, we're all responsible, Veronica was *our* shipmate as well as yours – rather detracts from the lust for life.'

'We can discuss ethics later. Get the rockets out.'

'Let me finish. I don't know how George and Jim feel about it, Alan, but my guess is that their sentiments are the same as mine. Meanwhile, it's pretty obvious what's happened. When we got away from the machine world Veronica managed to stave off dissolution by sheer will-power. And then, all the time, she kept kidding herself that she had something to live for. She was kidding herself when she offered the body beautiful in exchange for the charts, and as long as the feeling of exaltation that usually goes with sacrifices lasted she stayed in one piece. When that exaltation wore off she had nothing to keep her going. She let go.

'And Baron Bligh found that he had nothing to keep his bed warm, but a rag and a bone and a hank of hair – a rag of decaying plastic, a fathom or so of spun nylon, a huddle of aluminium bones. And Bligh's annoyed and, by his lights, justifiably so. And Bligh, now that his barrage has drawn no return fire, is certain that the ship's unarmed. He'll be coming after you in person.'

'That's what I've been trying to tell you.'

'I still haven't finished. I just want to make this clear. We shall fight to save the ship and to save our own skins, but certainly not to save *yours*. But the real reason why we shall fight is that Veronica bought the charts for us, and we'd hate her not to get her money's worth. That's all.'

In the light from the airlock I could see that Alan's face was white. He said, 'All right. Just get the rockets out. And get a pair of night glasses down here, but don't open fire until I give the word.'

We broke out our six remaining signal rockets and stacked them neatly to one side of the projector. Alan ran a loudspeaker on an extension lead from the control room to the airlock. From the airlock ran the cable supplying current to the rocket projector, the power that would, when the button was pressed, ignite the chemical propellant. The lead of the firing button, however, was taken to one side; there could be no rapid reloading if the rocketeers were to have to keep running back into the relative safety of the ship. We rehearsed our drill. It was very rough and ready, but we hoped that it would suffice.

Alan went back to his control room. The huge binoculars there were far more efficient than the small pair that I was using. I gained the impression of some sort of confused activity around the gates, of shadows passing and re-passing in front of the light, but that was all.

Alan's voice crackled from the speaker, 'Cavalry massing for the charge.'

Balancing my glasses atop the launching tube I trained the weapon to the bearing on which I thought I saw the greatest movement.

'Stand by,' remarked Alan.

'I wish he'd shut up,' said Dudley.

There was something advancing towards us. It reminded me of a dark river in spate, a river that tossed on the crests of its waves all manner of debris. But the dark shafts upraised against the glow of light from the town were not relatively harmless tree trunks and branches, but lances. I decided that I had no desire to be skewered. I glanced to one side, saw Dudley crouching there with the firing switch in his hand. The sight was as frightening as that of the advancing cavalry. I had no desire to be incinerated and incinerated I should be if I were not clear when Dudley pressed the button.

Even so, I kept my crude sights on the enemy.

I heard Alan say sharply, 'Fire!'

It was my intention to jump to one side but I tripped on a root. I fell, then rolled frantically over the rough ground. I heard the screaming roar as the big rocket left the tube, felt a blast of heat. I raised my head, saw that the missile had passed over the cavalry, was on trajectory for the hill on which stood the castle. I didn't wait to see it hit. I scrambled to my feet, ran over the burning heath to the projector. The tripod had fallen on its side. Working desperately Dudley and I got it standing again, then pushed another of the rockets into and up the breech.

My glasses were still hanging on their landyard about my neck. One lens was useless, cracked and dirt-smeared. The other one was usable. I looked for a target, found none. I noticed, almost with disinterest, that in the distant town the castle was burning.

'They scattered,' came Alan's voice, faint and distorted. The loudspeaker had caught the back-blast. 'They scattered, but they're re-grouping. To the left of the town. To the left . . .'

I could see them now, although not so clearly as before. My binoculars were damaged and, furthermore, the riders were not in silhouette against the town light. But I traversed the launching tube and, this time, tried to allow a little less elevation, keeping it pointed, so far as I was able, at the ground just ahead of the charge.

'Stand by,' said Alan superfluously.

I thought, *He's letting the bastards get close.* I thought of those long, vicious lances.

'*Fire!*'

This time when I jumped, I did not trip. The rocket, when it was clear of the tube, seemed to travel with agonising slowness. There was time, there had to be time, for the leading riders to pull out and clear. But time is relative, especially subjective time. Bligh's cavalry was on a collision course with the missile and, inevitably, the collision happened. Collision? Catastrophe, rather. By the light of the flaring exhaust we saw men and animals, pieces of men and animals, flung up and to all sides. The rocket, leaving a burning trail behind it, skimmed the ground, zigzagging now and again when deflected by some obstruction, finally vanished low on the horizon.

When it was gone we heard the screaming. My imagination got to work and I was stooped over, vomiting, when Dudley shook me and pulled me to the overset projector. Together we struggled to right the thing.

Something whined past us, and something else struck the metal tripod with a sharp *ping*, the shock jarring my hands unpleasantly. From all sides came a harsh, intermittent rattling noise. I looked up and saw that the night was suddenly alive with fireflies.

Dudley cursed, pulled me away from the stubborn launching tube. He pushed me into the shell crater, followed me.

Overhead the tracer from Bligh's ancient machine rifles made pretty patterns against the black sky.

'What,' I demanded, 'do we do now?'

'We could,' said Dudley, 'make a break for the air-lock.'

'There's a lull in the firing . . .'

'I don't suppose that the riflemen want to waste ammo,' he said. He scrabbled in the dirt, found a long root with a large clod of earth still adhering to it. He lifted it carefully above the crater rim, clod end uppermost. There was a vicious rattle of fire, a stream of tracer, and the clod disintegrated. He said, 'But they'll shoot when there's anything to shoot at.'

'So what do we do? Wait?'

'Looks like it.'

'If Alan had the sense to switch off the floods we might stand a chance.'

'Alan,' he said, 'hasn't shown much sense of late.' He added, 'That bitch!'

'Veronica? But . . .'

'Are we thinking of the same Veronica?' he countered.

Then we heard Alan's voice from the speaker. 'George,' he said. 'Dudley. Hold on.'

'Isn't that nice of him?' I growled.

I crawled up the side of the crater, peered over the rim. As I watched, the outer door of the airlock slid shut, although the external floodlights still cast their hard radiance around the ship. Then there was a flicker of flame under the main venturi. I cried out, incautiously exposed my head. A burst of tracer made me duck hurriedly.

I cried, 'Damn him, he's shut the door. He's shut the door. And old Jim must have the pump fixed, so now he's warming up the Drive. First Veronica, and now us . . . Dudley, just how low can a man sink?'

'Wait,' said Dudley.

'But I've told you what he's doing. The pump's repaired. He's warming up the Drive. He's leaving us, Dudley. He'll sacrifice anybody to his blasted dream!'

'Wait,' said Dudley.

The gentle coughs of the warming up blasts ceased

abruptly, then there was a sustained roaring. I knew what was happening, although I dared not expose myself to watch. I could visualise the bright flower of flame blooming under *Lucky Lady*'s stern. I could imagine her lifting up and away, diminishing until she was no more than a fast fading star in the black sky. The one thing that made no sense was old Jim's playing along with Alan. But perhaps he thought that we were safely aboard, or had been told that we were dead.

The ship was in sight now from our shellhole but, although fireborne, she was not lifting. She hung there, balanced delicately atop the incandescent pillar of her screaming exhaust. I found that I was hoping fiercely that the pump was failing again, that she would fall, that Jim and Alan would share whatever fate it was that Baron Bligh or his successor had in mind for us. I regretted these thoughts later, but when one is convinced that one has been sold down the river a certain bitterness is understandable.

Then she moved out of our field of vision. She moved not upwards, but laterally. We heard, but faintly, a frenzied burst of machine rifle fire. We heard, perhaps, a thin, high screaming. Down the wind drifted the reek of burning vegetable matter, of burning flesh.

Dudley shouted excitedly and scrambled out of the crater. I followed him. I saw, then, what Alan was doing. With the immobilisation of our rocket projector the ship had no weapons, but Alan was using the ship herself as a weapon. Slowly, methodically, he was ranging back and forth, using the auxiliary jets to induce lateral drift, reducing the heathland beneath the main exhaust to glowing embers. We saw dark figures break and run as that flaming sword was about to smite them. We saw them, briefly, dancing terribly in the torrent of incandescent gases.

Enough, I was thinking. *Enough. Surely this is enough.*

Lucky Lady paused, lifted. Then slowly, inexorably, she began to glide back to where we were standing. We waved frantically. Surely Alan would recognise us, would not think that we were two of the Baron's men. We were ready to turn and run when we saw that she was dropping. She grounded gently, only a few yards from where we were standing. The airlock door opened, the ramp was extended.

Thankfully we ran to the shelter of the ship.

Chapter Fourteen

Time is relative.

Objectively, the voyage from the pirates' lair did not take long. Subjectively it should not have taken long. We had plenty to occupy our time; we had to work hard and continuously to make the necessary modifications to those almost hopelessly out-of-date star charts.

Subjectively it should not have taken long, but it did. We missed Veronica – old Jim Dudley and myself. We missed her, and we hated Alan for having let her go, and we hated ourselves for having allowed Alan to barter her for a handful of archaic charts. The atmosphere in the ship was strained and tense, all the more so since the three of us had made it clear to our captain that we were withdrawing from the enterprise as soon as we grounded at Port Farewell.

The tension eased slightly when, at long last, the world of Faraway loomed huge in our viewports. Alan was happy now that he was home, or almost home, with the bright lights of Port Farewell a luminous blur against the darkness of the night side of the planet, with the familiar voice of Captain Wallis, the Port Master, crackling from the transceiver and telling us to land at will.

We came in on Ehrenhaft Drive, hitting the atmosphere at a shallow angle, the first few molecules of Faraway's gaseous envelope setting up a thin, high keening as they rushed past and around every irregularity of our hull. We came in, and short blasts from our auxiliary rockets turned us so that we were stern on to the still distant surface.

It was Reaction Drive then, the gingerly-made descent down the long column of incandescence, the sort of landing for which the ship had never been designed – but the sort of landing that, with a master hand at the controls, she was quite capable of making . . .

. . . until the propellant pump stripped the blades of the impeller.

Kemp did not hesitate.

'Take over, Dudley,' he snapped. 'You're as good a rocket pilot as I am. George, tell Jim to get the manual pump working. Tell him I'll be right down!'

Then we fell.

How far we fell, I cannot say. All I know is this – the dark globe below us was expanding with terrifying rapidity. Then, suddenly, the rockets coughed twice, coughed a third time and then broke into a full throated roar. That was when old Jim Larsen came into Control. 'Alan chased me out,' he complained. 'He wants all hands in the safest part of the ship. I left him in the engineroom, sweating away at the hand pump.'

'And you left him,' I said accusingly.

'Yes, I left him.' He went on softly, 'Don't you understand? He has to do this. It's his way of wiping out all that's happened. It has to be this way, otherwise he'll never be able to live with himself again.'

We fell, but under control. Dudley used rocket power

sparingly. His technique, in the circumstances, was a sound one – the employment of maximum braking blast at almost the last moment. It should have worked. It would have worked with new, or almost new, rocket motors. But the strain on the already cracked firing chambers was too great and the main venturi gave up just when it should have been our tower of strength, and for the second – and the last – time in her life *Lucky Lady* crashed disastrously.

The emergency organisation at Port Farewell is efficient.

I have a faint memory of screaming sirens, of great blades slicing through our shell plating as though it were paper, of willing hands dragging old Jim, Dudley and myself from the wreckage. Rather to my own surprise, and in spite of all attempts to restrain me, I was able to stand up, to stagger towards the crumpled stern. Somebody was asking me, 'How many of a crew have you? Where are the others?'

'Just one more,' I told him. 'The Captain. In the engineroom.'

They got Alan out. He was badly cut and burned, and there were bones broken, but he was conscious. 'George,' he said faintly. 'Veronica . . . Tell Veronica . . .' Then, 'Is she here?'

'No.'

'Ring her . . . Tell her I'm . . . all right . . .'

They carried him off and somehow forgot about me. I wandered into the administration building, went to the nearest telephone. I didn't need to look up the number. I pressed the correct sequence of buttons, waited. The little screen above the instrument remained dark and there was that most desolate of all sounds, the ringing of a telephone bell in an empty house. I checked the number in the book, found that my memory had not been faulty, then tried again, fruitlessly.

I remembered, as one does remember comparatively trivial things in times of crises, that there was money, Rim Worlds currency, in my pocket. I wandered out of the office to the cab rank. There were a dozen ground cars there and I got into the first one, giving the driver Alan's address.

He was one of those talkative cabbies.

He said, 'Seems to have been a crash at the port. I could see the ship coming in. A damn fool who handles a ship like that isn't fit to be in charge of a kiddy car, let alone a starwagon.'

He said, 'Did you see the crash, Mister?'

He said, 'Any idea what ship it was, Mister?'

He said, at last, 'You're here, Mister. And thanks for the scintillating conversation.'

I got out, paid him and ran up the short drive to the front door. The house was in darkness. Even so, I rang the bell. Then I hammered on the door. Then I rang the bell again.

I was aware that a woman was looking at me over the low hedge that divided Alan's garden from the neighbouring property.

She asked, 'Were you wanting Mrs Kemp?'

I said, 'Yes. Have you any idea where she is? When she'll be back?'

'I've no idea,' she told me. 'Earth, maybe. Or Caribbea. But she'll not be back.'

I reached across the hedge and grabbed her shoulder. I think that I must have shaken her. She squealed indignantly. 'Keep your hands to yourself, young man!' She looked at me closely in the dim light. 'But you're not Mr Kemp. What's it to you where Mrs Kemp is?'

'I'm Mr Kemp's friend. He was badly hurt in the crash out at the spaceport. I have to tell his wife.'

'She's gone,' she informed me with gloomy satisfaction. 'Weeks ago. There was a big ship in – *Aeriel* was her name. No, not the Shakespearian Line's *Aeriel*; this one was one of the Trans-Galactic Clippers, on a cruise. There was this man from the *Aeriel* – one of the passengers. He and Mrs Kemp seemed to be old friends. Can't say that I altogether blame her; he was tall, good looking, lots of money . . .'

'Has she gone?' I yelled.

'Yes, she's gone, as I've been trying to tell you for the last half hour. And don't shout at me, young man!'

Chapter Fifteen

The surgeons and the plastic surgeons patched Alan up very nicely.

But neither the surgeons nor the pyschiatrists, for all their fancy jargon, can mend a broken dream.

So that was the end of the dream.

Lucky Lady was a total loss, worth only her value in scrap. And she was not insured. She had brought us nothing in the way of riches – unless you count experience as riches, and some experiences should be chalked up on the debit rather than the credit side of the slate.

Rim Runners , who are always short of officers, took us back with no loss of rank or seniority. They did not, however, have Alan's services for long. He made an excellent physical recovery from his injuries but he was accident prone. A few weeks after his return to service he walked under a conveyor belt that he could just as easily have walked around, and a heavy ingot of zinc fell from the belt and killed him instantly.

I run into Dudley Hill now and again. He is now

Second Mate of *Rimtiger*; and old Jim Larsen and I are serving together in *Rimlion*. *Rimlion* is running the Eastern Circuit. She was on Tharn not so long ago, and Jim and I went ashore together to sample the local brew.

He was in a talkative mood, was old Jim. He was in a philosophical mood and, like most of his cloth, like practically all those who work with the Mannschenn Drive and are exposed to its time twisting fields, has rather weird ideas about Space and Time.

'Out on the Rim,' he said seriously, 'and especially on worlds such as this, planets that human beings have reached only within the past few decades, the Barrier must be very thin . . .'

'What Barrier?' I asked.

'The Barrier between the alternative time tracks, the divergent world lines . . .'

'Surely you don't believe . . .'

'And why shouldn't I?' He paused, losing interest in his dimensional theories. 'That girl,' he told me, pointing with his pipe stem at a red-head who had just come into the tavern, 'reminds me of Sally.' He caught her eye. She smiled, started to make her way to our table.

I left him then. I'm not prudish, but people of Tharn, although definitely humanoid, are not human. So I left him to it and walked slowly back, along the rough dirt road, to the spaceport.

The berthing area was the way that it usually is, a pattern of bright lights and deep shadows. Even so, I cannot see how this pattern can have produced the illusion of a peg-top-shaped hull, balanced upon its pointed end. It cannot possibly have produced the illusion of two figures, Captain and Captain's lady – and which Veronica was it? – walking arm in arm, up the ramp to the yellow-lit circle of the airlock. And the most impossible illusion of all, perhaps, was that of the man who stood there to greet them. I saw his face plainly as I approached, just before the odd scene winked out into nothingness.

It was my own.

Chapter Sixteen

When the dreamer dies, what of the dream?